Taxi: A Tribute to Harry Chapin

Authored by: *David W. Trapp*

Trapp Family Publishing LLC

Taxi: A Tribute to Harry Chapin

Copyright 2017: David W. Trapp

ISBN-13: 978-0-9800946-9-5
ISBN-10: 0980094690

2

This book, stuffed toy animals based on the *Daxton and Miranda Adventure Books*, additional books, research papers and other interesting items of note can all be discovered and purchased at:

WWW.AMAZON.COM

Other Books Written by
David W Trapp:

A Conservative Terrorist: *The Demise of Walter Reed*

Plates of Gold and Other Spiritual Poems

The $45,000 Cat

The Donkey and the Elephant

David's Youth Series:

"Miraculous Majesty Flies Again"
A Daxton and Miranda Adventure

"Tipsy Russell Recovers"
A Daxton and Miranda Adventure

"Army Dill Gets Shelled"
A Daxton and Miranda Adventure

"Kitty Gets Leveled"
A Daxton and Miranda Adventure

"Tom Turkey Gets Pardoned"
A Daxton and Miranda Adventure

"Rudolph Jr. Misses the Roof"
A Daxton and Miranda Adventure

"Topsail Turtle"
A Daxton and Miranda Adventure

In tribute to Harry Chapin, *"songwriter and storyteller extraordinaire"*; this book is dedicated to all those people who love his music! The book is also dedicated to Dede and only she knows why.

Taxi (1972)
Written and Composed by:
Harry Chapin (1942 – 1981)

It was raining hard in 'Frisco
I needed one more fare to make my night
A lady up ahead waved to flag me down
She got in at the light
Oh, where you going to, my lady blue
It's a shame you ruined your gown in the rain
She just looked out the window, she said
"Sixteen Parkside Lane"
Something about her was familiar
I could swear I'd seen her face before
But she said, "I'm sure you're mistaken"
And she didn't say anything more
It took a while, but she looked in the mirror
And she glanced at the license for my name
A smile seemed to come to her slowly
It was a sad smile, just the same

And she said, "How are you Harry?"
I said, "How are you Sue?
Through the too many miles
And the two little smiles
I still remember you"
It was somewhere in a fairy tale
I used to take her home in my car
We learned about love in the back of the Dodge
The lesson hadn't gone too far
You see, she was gonna be an actress
And I was gonna learn to fly
She took off to find the footlights
And I took off to find the sky

Whoa, I've got something inside me
To drive a princess blind
There's a wild man, wizard
He's hiding in me, illuminating my mind

Oh, I've got something inside me
Not what my life's about
'Cause I've been letting my outside tide me
Over 'till my time, runs o
Baby's so high that she's skying
Yes she's flying, afraid to fall
I'll tell you why baby's crying
'Cause she's dying, aren't we all
There was not much more for us to talk about
Whatever we had once was gone
So I turned my cab into the driveway
Past the gate and the fine trimmed lawns
And she said we must get together
But I knew it'd never be arranged
And she handed me twenty dollars
For a two fifty fare, she said
"Harry, keep the change"
Well, another man might have been angry
And another man might have been hurt
But another man never would have let her go
I stashed the bill in my shirt
And she walked away in silence
It's strange, how you never know
But we'd both gotten what we'd asked for
Such a long, long time ago
You see, she was gonna be an actress
And I was gonna learn to fly
She took off to find the footlights
I took off for the sky
And here, she's acting happy
Inside her handsome home
And me, I'm flying in my taxi
Taking tips, and getting stoned
I go flying so high, when I'm stoned

"It was raining hard in 'Frisco"

It was raining hard that late September evening in downtown San Francisco; a steady deluge of warm rainwater marched like lock-stepped tin soldiers directly off the nearby broiling ocean and poured down from the overloaded black clouds that rumbled their dark cadence overhead.

I had watched the impending storm approach throughout the laconic afternoon, and I knew that the transportation business I was engaged in would be either as slow as a seven-year itch that evening, or the constraining wet, dreary rain would invoke some ancient human desire to cleanse oneself in Mother Nature's natural shower, with the resulting cleansed commerce picking up substantially. I hoped it was the latter rather than the former – I needed the funds to pay for sustenance and residence.

The enveloping water engulfed my dull yellow chariot as I concentrated dismally on observing the night's events.

I observed the puddled streets through the bright glass that was holding the evening storm at bay as the worn-down windshield wipers catatonically and rhythmically pushed the rainwater from one side of the vehicle to the other.

You couldn't tell it right then because of the heavy weight and rate of the rain, but there would have been dirty, disgusting streaks on the windshield if the liquid had been any lighter in substance; the wipers were in even worse shape than the rest of the vehicle.

It would have been an easy and relatively inexpensive venture to replace the frazzled and dried out windshield wipers, but the dowdy and dreary owner of the cab company, a real cheapskate, wasted little time worrying about such things as wiper blades for his vehicles. Instead of doing his job, he concentrated on the daily betting sheet he carried with him constantly.

As a racetrack aficionado, the cab company's owner was a man who knew more about horses, and horseracing, than any other person alive.

At least he would inform you of that imagined superiority with little or no provocation. Not that his imaginary horse sense, track experience or knowledge of spirited and professionally-trained equines did him any good; he lost every time he went to the track, or so it seemed to me anyway. He was constantly griping and lamenting the fact that his "sure things" were only sure things to lose.

By the way, my name is Harry; I'm a wannabe songwriter and singer, and I drive a taxi because I really don't wish to starve to death. I'm not half-bad as a singer, even if I do say so myself (and I do).

My songs tend to be ballads and stories that are the stockpiled results stemming from my life experiences; some of those experiences have been good, many have been bad.

A few of my life experiences have contained intriguing possibilities for future considerations, and a handful have been beautifully impressed upon my soul. The story I am currently relating to you is one of those adventures that just has to be told.

My mind works in terms of romantically influenced poetic prose and rhymes. I have a quirky sense of humor that influences and guides the words, phrases, thoughts, rhymes and metered cadence of many of the hundreds of songs and poems that I have written throughout my life.

Even as a young child, my objective in life was to be an author, poet, songwriter, but most of all; a pilot.

I have a small cadre of fans, and when I'm not driving my taxi, I keep myself busy singing in the bars and clubs that cater to those who enjoy the local 'Frisco nightlife.

The other cab drivers I associate with tease me about making it to the big time; but, a majority of these fellow workers also like my songs and enjoy hearing me sing. I figure that those who do not like my songs are just braindead individuals with no artistic or musical appreciation anyway.

I just penned one of my favorites (so far); it's a song about a truckload of bananas spread all over the road.

I call it *30,000 pounds of bananas*; it's a popular tune and one that I enjoy singing in front of a raucous crowd who love to sing it along with me.

Every time I walk by one of my fellow taxi-cab drivers, either in the taxi-driver's bullpen or just walking by, one of them grins at me, says "smashed bananas" and shakes his head.

I know at least one of them has a copy of the song and I would bet they all listen to it at least once every day.

I'm still a devout single man at the ripe old age of thirty-one, much to the chagrin of my overly-sensitive mother, who is patiently awaiting the conception and birth (the birth more than the conception of course) of her first grandchild. She is slowly losing hope that either event will happen anytime soon.

I tell my mother that I'm waiting to hit the big time and then I'll have my choice of the litter (she's appalled when I refer to women in that manner).

Not that I wouldn't mind being happily married, it's just not high on my priority list right now, I want to concentrate on my career and not on taking on the responsibilities, duties and obligations of the all-encompassing job of marriage.

I don't need a wife right now, or any of the progenerated little rug-rats that might drop from heaven as a result of a night of good, clean marital sexual interaction.

Don't get me wrong, I have had my share of close relationships and clingy girlfriends throughout the years, and maybe a couple of them might have turned out to have been "the one"; that is if I had been even remotely interested; but, I had not been. I was far too busy with other more important goals and objectives.

In retrospect however, there was this girl that I met while lazily completing my high school years; she was a stunner, both mentally and physically. For a while, I thought I had found true love, but it was short-lived.

I don't remember what happened, I just remember that the result was the same as many of my relationships best described as 'here today, gone tomorrow."

I seem to recall that she went off to California to be an actress, and I was just devastated when she left me.

For as long as I remember, I have always wanted to be a famous songwriter, that goal, that objective, has always been right up there at the top of my life's plans, along with my goal of being a pilot.

I wanted to be a pilot who traveled the world on a daily basis, seeing things from the sky that other earth-bound humans could only dream of. I had almost given up on my fantasy of becoming a pilot; but I was damn sure that I was not going to achieve my chimera of being a singer/songwriter; I may not have reached that destination yet, but I would.

It seems to me that I have these beautiful, brilliant, and sometimes crazy songs in my head trying to burst their way out. The songs and words were always trying their very best to impress the world with their suavity and verve.

I must get these songs out of my head and presented to the public before I go batshit crazy; I truly don't think a wife would understand that.

Most of the women I've made acquaintance with only desire a man's devotion be totally concentrated on them.

The vast majority of these women want a man to focus on their needs and their concupiscence, not on a man's need to write songs and poems that don't generate significant compensation nor provide for food on the table.

I turned my attention back to the rain, wondering if it was going to keep up all night. "It was raining hard in Frisco," I sang softly to myself. Hey, I could write a song about the rain.

I laughed to myself, and thought, that's the most used cliché of all time. A song about the rain, I wonder how it would go?

I whistled aimlessly to myself as I turned left onto Geary Boulevard from Park Presidio Blvd.

I kept my eyes peeled for anyone needing transportation as I traveled leisurely east towards Union Square.

Theaters and shops around the Civic Center would be closing soon; there was a good chance I could grab a customer or two to help fill the empty coffers of the wallet lying next to me between the worn front seats in the tiny space I usually reserved for all my paperwork and trash.

I listened to the rain as it drummed on the taxi's roof overhead and thought about my life, my needs, and making it to the *big time*.

"*I needed one more fare to make my night*"

Ahead on the right was a young couple hurriedly entering a white mini-van with the assistance of an older man wearing a turban and holding an umbrella over their heads. "Non-union workers strike again" I thought to myself dejectedly, then laughed at the irony of my thought.

Ever since the introduction of non-union taxi-cab drivers, my business had plummeted. I'm a devout capitalist, so I understand how it works, I just wish we could go back to the time when taxi services were a monopoly; that way I could make more money in less time and not have to work as hard for it.

I laughed to myself as I cherished the concept of a devout capitalist thinking socialistic thoughts. How ironic! I guess that might be how a lot of poor people think, and maybe they have a right to. I just can't handle socialism.

I would rather have an opportunity to be wealthy through my own efforts, even if I ended up dirt poor, than to have a government that made all my decisions for me; I just see a total lack of personal control in that situation.

What I really should do is get a nice vehicle of my own and drive for myself. If I drove for myself, I could keep more of the money I earned, and I would get a new vehicle of my very own instead of this piece of crap taxi that sometimes felt as if it was ready to give up the ghost at any second.

Either way, capitalist or socialist, I still had to concentrate on making enough money to pay the rent this month; it was coming due at the end of the week.

My previous wish about today's weather had not been fulfilled, the pouring rain had slowed business; I needed at least one more fare to make worthy my effort of showing up to work.

I had a formula, well not really a formula, more like a guideline, (kind of reminds me of the pirate's code in that Johnny Depp movie when the girl asks for parlay) that I employed to determine whether driving a taxi was worthwhile or whether I should just go flip burgers at the local Castro Burger joint.

My goal in driving a taxi was to earn enough money on an hourly basis to cover my fixed expenses.

If I could cover my fixed expenses, then I could use the money I earned from my entertainment gigs to further my singing and songwriting career.

At some point, I hoped to give up the taxi driving career, but I was not quite there yet, especially if I wished to continue to eat.

I hoped I would reach the point of no return soon; maybe then I could think about the entire marriage and family scenario. Maybe.

"It was raining hard in Frisco," I hummed to myself. "I needed one more fare to make my night".

Oh yeah, the opening stanza; the beginnings of a song percolated in the back of my mind; phrases bubbling slowly to the surface.

I grinned at no one as a well-liked and a very welcome process initiated itself within me.

Some of my best songs had been created in this same manner. I shivered eagerly with anticipation of a new creation.

"A lady up ahead waved to flag me down (she got in at the light)"

I approached Union Square from the west; it was my objective to swing by the Hilton Convention Center, perhaps picking up a late-night passenger needing a ride to the airport, or a businessman too inebriated to drive himself home. I studiously scanned the sidewalks for the telltale signal of a rider in need.

Ahead on the right, I spied an individual huddling in a shop doorway who was holding an umbrella overhead in a futile effort to shield the drenching rain.

She must have recognized the lighted *vacant* sign atop my taxi because she stepped out into the torrent as I neared her location. She hurriedly waved her hand at me to ensure that I saw her.

I responded by pulling my taxi out of the slow-moving traffic, accelerating my vehicle to quickly reach her and then slowing as I neared her location.

I certainly did not wish to add to the lady's discomfort by splashing water on her; she seemed wet enough already from the downpour. As I stopped directly adjacent to her, she stepped from the curb and hurriedly opened the back door to the taxi.

She slid wetly, yet elegantly, into my vehicle with just a whisper of perfume; a perfume smell that piqued memories of long lost love, spring times, blossoming flowers, and a cool brisk wind blowing through the freshly leavened aspens growing on a nearby mountainside.

The packages she carried with her she quickly threw onto the seat beside her.

My first glance at her darkened visage in the driver's mirror took in the fact that she was as bedraggled as a wet puppy, and she confirmed my prognosis by shaking her head in an aggressive manner to rid herself of the water dripping from her clothing and hair.

It seemed that her hair was blonde in color, but it looked a darker tint due to the weather. Even soaking wet, the lady was quite lovely.

I turned to look over the seat at her and she smiled ruefully at me while shrugging her shoulders in an expressive manner.

"I'm sorry about the water," she said.

Her voice caught me off guard, there was something about it that tickled my inner being; it was soft; melodious, a voice that flowed like fine whiskey over ice, filling the glass with musical sounds to savor as they were sipped; it was a dark, dusky voice that was filled with promises and a quiet sexiness that sent shivers up my spine.

I had heard a voice like that in a previous life, but I could not specifically pinpoint the time or place.

"It's fine," I shrugged. "This car has seen a lot worse, that's for sure." I turned my head around to study the passing traffic.

23

I glanced at the traffic light overhead and watched as it blinked from a bright green to an amber red; I slowly eased my car into the traffic passing to my left.

It seemed to me that I had a special passenger and I must take care with my driving; I wanted to deliver this young princess to her ultimate destination in a safe manner.

"Oh, where you going to, my lady blue?"

I've often thought of myself as a modern-day Casanova (for those of you who have no clue as to what I speak, Giacomo Girolamo Casanova is a famous 18th century swain whose moniker has become highly associated with the word "womanizer").

I have an eye for beauty, and it works especially well with young females after they have sojourned into a wet, windy and rainy day spent shopping, working or sightseeing in San Francisco.

I glanced in the mirror at my soaked and still dripping passenger and smiled to myself; from what I could see; within the confines of the dark backseat of the vehicle, this lady rider was gorgeous, a real beauty to behold.

As we passed under the overhead streetlights, the scintillant output reflected through the windows, enhancing and obscuring her features in a cacophony of alternating light and darkness.

She seemed to have the type of face that bespoke of Athens, ancient Greece, Helen of Troy and Mark Anthony's love Cleopatra all rolled into one lifetime experience.

I wished silently that I could see her distinct features more clearly, but I did not want to turn and stare; that would have been too rude, too obvious.

I spoke up from my driver's seat. "So, where you headed lady?" She seemed lost in her own thoughts and when she did not immediately reply, I wondered to myself if she had even heard me.

"Oh, where you going to, my lady blue" I quipped to her in a casual fashion. She looked up at me, startled out of her reverie. I continued to glance at her reflection in the mirror over the dash but her face remained hidden from me.

"Would you just drive for now?" she asked. "I wish to think for a moment if that's okay."

I nodded my head in acquiescence and continued driving away from the Convention Center. I headed west on Geary Street towards Geary Boulevard.

Humming my new tune quietly to myself, I thought about adding a new line to the opening stanza; "oh where you going to my lady blue". I smiled; the song was beginning to take shape.

"It's a shame you ruined your gown in the rain"

From what I could see of her, this lady had class. She was wearing a dress that even a neophyte such as myself could see cost a pretty penny; though the dress currently hung from her frame in an unkempt manner due to the rain, it still emphasized her body in a subtle manner that an off-the-shelf dress could never compete with.

Her breasts were completely covered; the dress did not obscure them, instead her shape was enhanced by the fabric, accentuated in a under- spoken manner.

It had to be either a Wrap dress by Diane Von Furstenburg, or a Dulce Gabanna. Since it had a more classic appeal to it, and it showed her form without being too flashy, I determined it to be a Wrap.

I could not determine the exact color of the dress, most of the fabric was soaked through by the downpour; but no matter what the color, it was dark and clingy on her, and very sexy.

I felt bad for my passenger since a dress like that would likely cost more than what I would pay for a month's rent on my apartment. Of course, my apartment was on the shabby side, but still!

"It's a shame" I told her, "that you ruined your gown in the rain."

She looked up as I spoke, surprised that a taxi driver would say such a thing about the way she was dressed. In my defense, I had just written an article on the fashion industry and that was the only reason why I knew so much about what was currently fashionable in women's wear and how much it cost.

Oh, did I forget to tell you that I also used my writing skills to pen articles and research reports on various subjects? Yeah, well, I do. Writing is writing, and if I can make a few extra bucks using the creative skills God granted me, then who was I to pretend that I was too good for such endeavors? Besides, I like to write.

I risked a glance at her in the mirror and still could not see much; not a smile, not a frown, nothing. I closed my mouth; sometimes it's better to be thought a fool than it is to open your mouth and prove it true. We traveled forward in silence.

"It's a shame you ruined your gown in the rain,". Wow, that could be the next line in my song.

I ran through what I had composed in my head so far, and concentrated on adding in the next line to what I already had; yep, it worked. I laughed to myself at how easily words seem to flow together once they were initiated. It's always been that way for me, I have always been able to rhyme words, sing phrases, write pages, compose paragraphs and complete chapters; it just seems so natural to me.

I can write about anything; a perfect example is my before-mentioned banana song. I came up with the song by reading a story about a truck driver.

The semi-truck driver was traveling fast down I-80 through Pennsylvania and was going too fast. The driver missed a curve and the semi he was driving overturned.

His cargo was 30,000 pounds of bananas, and every single one of them spilled out onto the expressway.

Reading the story, I was immediately intrigued by the image of so many bananas obstructing a major highway.

Can you imagine 30,000 pounds of bananas on the roadway? Better yet, can you imagine cleaning up 30,000 pounds of bananas?

I just had to write a song about the event; surprisingly enough, it took me less than an hour to write it.

This new song in my head concerning my lady passenger seemed to be flowering in a similar fashion.

"She just looked out the window"

The rain continued in unrelenting fashion, and for a few moments I concentrated solely on my driving. Traffic had picked up somewhat and I did not wish to become another statistic.

Being in an accident costs money, time and aggravation that I did not need, nor desire. Not only that, but the taxi's owner would surely make me pay for any necessary (or even unnecessary) repairs to the vehicle. A little fender-bender could easily end up costing me more than this job was worth.

I glanced in the mirror and noticed that my lady blue was now staring resolutely out the window with her faced turned away from me.

I studied what little of her features I could see and was rewarded by an insight that surprised me; this lady was not the picture of happiness and joy. No, this lady was pensive as she stared out at the passing city sights.

Lights flickered through her drying hair, and I could see a slight hunch to her shoulders that displayed sadness along with a certain sense of defiance.

There was also a subtle strength that seemed to shine forth; an inner core that provided an unshakeable foundation for accomplishing great things.

Of course, that could be my wild imagination running free again, or perhaps it was just wishful thinking on my part.

I was constantly projecting my thoughts and idealistic concepts onto others, I'm a poet at heart, I guess.

I took another quick glimpse at her in my mirror but she continued to just look out the window, ignoring me, ignoring my quick glances.

She was probably used to male ogling, and chose to ignore it. Like I said, this lady had class. I still had no idea where she was heading, that was okay with me, especially with the meter running.

The longer we just drove around, the more money I would earn. The more money I earned, the closer to achieving my dreams. Or, I thought to myself, at least I can pay the rent for this month. I smiled to myself.

"She said, sixteen Parkside Lane"

Her euphonious voice overcame my introspection. I blinked, and said "what?" Looking out the window again, she said "Sixteen Parkside Lane, that's where I want to go".

I whistled silently to myself; Parkside Lane is located in one of San Fran's most famous, and one of its ritziest, gated communities.

The homes there could not really be called homes, mansions would be a much more appropriate term. It was no wonder this woman oozed class, either she, or her husband had a lot of money.

My tip was either going to be huge, or miniscule; you could never tell with these people with money, they usually gave big tips, but some of them were as miserly as Scrooge on his worst day.

I pointed my taxi west towards the Pacific Ocean and mused about Parkside Lane.

Sixteen Parkside Lane resonated loudly as part of my new song; it was a famous street; nestled right off Geary Boulevard and linking it to Point Lobos Avenue in the Sea Cliff neighborhood.

It was also one of San Fran's richest zip codes; the average income in that area of town was well into six figures.

San Francisco sport celebrities, local politicians and a variety of CEO's all maintained residences there. I wondered who this woman was that had stumbled her way to my taxicab; I looked in the mirror again to see if I could recognize her, but the back seat was still too dark to get a good look.

I continued west on Geary Boulevard towards the ocean. The rain continued to pour down upon the car, making a steady drumbeat of noise, drowning out the normal noises emanating from the vehicle.

Driving a taxi is so repetitive that it can be mind-numbing, but that can also be an advantage to a hopelessly romantic songwriter such as myself.

I did not even realize that I was still humming my latest work-in-progress, but there it was on the periphery of my thoughts.

I turned my focus to attempting to determine who this lady was.

My new song, however, infringed upon those thoughts with an insistence that was exciting.

The manner in which she voiced, "Sixteen Parkside Lane" made the words reverberate like a ping pong in my head.

I did not know whether I should concentrate on my lady blue sitting in the back seat, or on the song that was set to bloom in my head like a summer tulip in the early morning sunshine.

I glanced in the mirror once more but saw nothing new.

I returned to my thoughts; wondering to myself what it would be like to live in a mansion. As I was growing up, I had often dreamed of the time when I would become a famous song-writer and singer, of the time when women would be throwing themselves at me, when I made so much money, I wouldn't know what to do with it all, of the house on the oceanfront that I would buy, of the loving wife I would have that would adore me, support me with her love, and of the many gifts that I would shower on her.

I dreamed of having children that would worship me; the best father ever! I knew that I would have the time to spend with my son, that he and I would become best friends, playing catch, going to sporting events; the whole shebang.

I also dreamed of traveling the world, signing autographs, riding in the back seat of limos, of the many songs I would write. My house would be a mansion even bigger than the one that I was currently driving towards.

Of course, on the road of life that I was currently traveling, my dreaming might be the closest I ever come to achieving my mansion home.

I worried about that for a second, then I brightened up once more; this next song might be the one to put me over the top.

I mulled over the words as they sang through my head; this is what I had so far….it was raining hard in Frisco, I needed one more fare to make my night, a lady up ahead waved to flag me down, she got in at the light. I said, where you going to my lady blue, it's a shame you ruined your gown in the rain, she just looked out the window and said Sixteen Parkside Lane; it wasn't a bad start.

I looked in the mirror again and was rewarded with a full-on look at my passenger, the first clear look I was able to get.

"Something about her was familiar"

My breath caught in my throat; I had seen that look, those eyes, that face; there was something so familiar about her. Was her photo in a magazine? Was she someone famous? Just a month ago I had picked up Madonna at the airport, and even though she was dressed in a "normal" outfit, I had recognized her after only a few moments; was this lady someone famous as well? I looked again, but her face was obscured once more.

I took all that I knew so far about my rider and tried to put it all together.

Have you ever had that feeling that you should know someone, that you should recognize who they are, yet you are unable to do so?

Once in a while, I get experience these recognitions, and it drives me nuts until I figure out who they are; I wracked my brain in an effort to discern her identity.

This was going to bother me until I got an answer. I tried a trick that I was taught by my dad while I was still a young man.

My father once told me that if I wanted to remember something that I should let my thoughts wander onto something totally off the subject and that my brain would then be able to search my subconscious and would soon find the answer. So, I moved my thoughts back to my song and tried to write the next line.

"Something about her was familiar", it worried me that I could not discern what it was. Now don't get me wrong, I don't use the word "worried" in that I was concerned, I used it more along the lines of a dog worrying a bone.

I did have concerns about whether I had really become so mundane, so entrenched in my own life, my own worries, my own daily tasks that I could no longer remember people outside my little circle of daily friends and acquaintances; what does that say about my empathy for other individuals?

Would I become the songwriter that I truly believe I was meant to be, if I could not even discover a familiarity of sorts between myself and other people?

My thought process was on a tangent, a tangent that just might jog my memory into remembering who exactly this lady was reclining in the back seat of my taxi.

I still did not recall her identity, perhaps what I needed was a jolt of some kind, an impetus that would ignite the fire of recall in a way that I would benefit from it.

I continue to steal glances in the mirror to garner further details, but that did not work. Well, it's like my dad told me, just let it go for a while.

"I could swear I'd seen her face before"

Okay, I admit it; I could not let it go. This was about to drive me crazy, if I could see her face maybe that would help. I decided that I would take drastic measures, if I was careful she would not catch on concerning what I was attempting.

"I have to stop for a second if you don't mind" I spoke up from the driver's seat. "Is that okay with you?"

I looked for her reflection in the mirror as I broached my question. I was almost immediately rewarded with a full-on searching look as she faced forward and returned my look in the mirror. I had caught her at the most optimum moment as we entered a well-lit section of road at that exact second. There! I had it, I knew who she was, or at least I'm pretty sure that it was her.

"Why do you have to stop?" she questioned.

I glanced down at the dashboard before replying.

"Never mind," I told her. "My oil light had been flashing the last few moments, but it looks like it has stopped now".

She sat back and did not reply. I watched her for a few additional seconds before I ventured forth with my next comment, "I could swear I've seen your face before, are you famous…a movie star perhaps, a singer, maybe a comedian?"

She laughed softly, more to herself than in reply to my query. "I wish," she replied. "But, no I am not any of those, just an average woman living an average life."

"Hmmm," I returned. "Now I'm going to sit and wonder where I have seen you."

She glanced in the mirror again, and once more I was provided with a brief glimpse. I was more positive now than I was after the first look.

"You really do look like someone very familiar to me," I told her. "I could swear I've seen your face before."

She did not reply, and I closed my mouth.

I had done what I could, now the next step was up to her.

"She said; I'm sure you're mistaken (and she didn't say anything more)"

She glanced away from the window and the passing scenery and said to me, "I'm sure you are mistaken."

I was disappointed, perhaps she was not really who I thought she was. Perhaps, my romantic side was overcoming my commonsense side. It would certainly not be the first time that I had romanticized a relationship with a beautiful passenger.

It was the first time I felt so strongly that I had known a rider from my past though. I did not say anything, and decided to keep my thoughts to myself.

If she thought I was mistaken, then she was entitled to her opinion. My self-esteem would take the hit, I thought to myself. After all, I was not positive that it was her, well not entirely positive anyway; probably about 85%. I continued to catch glimpses of her face in the mirror as we traveled closer to her home. "Is your husband famous maybe?" I questioned her.

"He is a movie director," she replied. "A lot of people know him."

"That could be it!" I paused as I caught her attention. "Could I have seen a picture of you in the newspaper with him?"

She answered reluctantly. "Yes, I often have to attend parties and events with him. I don't really like to, but duty calls." She gave a rueful chuckle. "That's where I was tonight when you picked me up. I left early and did not want to take the car, or have our driver take me home. I wanted to do some shopping and have a few moments for myself for once."

"I understand," I commiserated. "I like being alone sometimes as well. Doesn't everyone?"

A hint of a smile crossed her face. "I guess." She turned her face to the window, but now that I had her talking, I wasn't willing to let the conversation go.

"What type of event was it?" I questioned.

She did not answer right away. I waited patiently and was eventually rewarded. "It was a benefit for a local charity that helps kids."

"Oh, that's nice. Do you have any kids?"

"No." Her reply was succinct and brush. She must have felt badly about her rejoinder as she immediately explained, "I like kids, we just never had any."

Her remark revealed the fact that the subject of children might be a touchy issue for her; I carefully tried to steer away from it but before I could she turned the subject around on me.

"What about you?" she asked. "Are you married? Do you have any children?"

"No," I replied. "I'm not married yet. And, no children that I know of."

"Yet?" she queried. "Does that mean you plan on it anytime soon?"

"No, I'm dating but nothing serious. I don't think anyone can put up with me, long term." I laughed.

She smiled and emitted a small chuckle. "I'm sure there is someone out there for you" and then she didn't say anything more.

I loved her laugh, her chuckle, her smile and I had once loved more than that. I was now one hundred percent sure that she was who I thought she was.

Her name was Susan Littleton, or at least it used to be Susan Littleton. I knew her as Sue. We had been lovers once, boyfriend and girlfriend, two ships traveling the same ocean, coupled by more than just a refueling cord. In the muddled masses of society's convoy, we were a battleship and a destroyer, both plowing through heavy waters dependent on each other on the heavy seas of life.

I wondered if I should tell her, but decided to remain silent for now; don't ask me why, but I was taking a wait-and-see approach. I've always been rather reluctant in relationships.

I wasn't sure whether she would remember me, or if she did remember me, if it would be a good or bad thing.

Sue had been my very first true love, and there was always something special about your first love. Most people never, ever forgot their first love. I know I had not done so, and I was surprised by the amount of pain and anguish that suddenly surfaced once again as I recalled our parting.

"It took a while, but she looked in the mirror"

I continued driving the route leading towards her destination but slowed the vehicle somewhat; I told myself that it was due to the rain that continued to pour down on the car, but in reality, I was slowing down to give her and myself a little more time together.

I told you that I was a romantic sort of man, even now thoughts were running through my head as I reminisced about my past with Sue. The good times, and the bad.

The thoughts continued to bombard me, and I reveled in the process. I did not say anything to her, but I did look in the mirror on a frequent basis, a couple of times I caught her eyes looking in the mirror in the same manner as I was; her attempt to discern who I was.

Perhaps I had piqued her interest? Her eyes caught mine once more, and I endured a piercing look from her. Did I see a hint of recognition in those eyes?

I was not sure of what I saw; I could only hope. I reached up and adjusted the mirror in a calculated mien, and our eyes met again. I felt sure of it now; she recognized me, or so I hoped.

I can be such a romantic; sometimes, I shock even myself. I often make it a point to remember special events and dates that are important to the person that I am with at that specific time of my life.

Many of my girlfriends have been surprised by the attention I show them, and they embrace the fact that I don't forget the little things that make a relationship important.

My advice to anyone reading my story is to treasure those individuals that you love, especially since they may not be around as long as you think they will; I know that from experience. I don't wish to be maudlin or gothic in nature, but I've experienced many losses in my life, and some of them have been permanent in nature.

"And she glanced at the license for my name"

I looked at her once more and saw that she was looking at the license dangling from the dashboard. I was suddenly glad that it was a state law that every taxicab driver had to display his license in the vehicle. The picture on the license was not one that I was especially proud of, but at least it was recognizable as me, and the license displayed my name in big, bold letters.

What I hoped for, was that Sue would be able to read my name from the back seat, especially in a relatively dark environment.

The streetlights we passed under continued to ply the inside of the vehicle in intermittent phosphorescence, but I was not sure that it was enough for her to discern my name. I watched her in the mirror as she glanced at the license again. Was there something there? I wasn't sure, but it seemed that way.

Our eyes were meeting on a more
frequent basis, I could feel the atmosphere
in the enclosed environment of the
vehicle ratchet up two or three notches.

My song added another expression to the
verse; "she glanced at the license for my
name.? I smiled to myself, the song was
starting to come together.

Have you ever had a time in your life
when events rolled forward through no
extra effort of your own?

That's what this song, and this lady in my
taxi seemed to be doing; they were going
hand-in-hand, and I was just along for the
ride.

By glancing at my license for my name,
she was displaying the same curious
nature that I was experiencing.

"A smile seemed to come to her slowly"

There, there it was! I saw it, an alluring smile appeared on her face, slowly lighting the entire cab with its presence. Had I ever seen anything so beautiful, so commanding through its simplicity? I doubt that I had, or that I would ever see such a sight again. My entire being radiated in response to that one loving, caring, compassionate smile. Gorgeous, is the word that came to mind, and I was immediately enlightened, and chagrined.

It was a smile that I remembered very well, and I could hardly take a breath without realizing just how much I missed seeing that smile, sharing its warmth, basking in its glow that emanated so strongly from the lovely lady wearing it in such a unique way.

Describing her smile brings back a flood of memories, beautiful memories filled with love, joy, happiness and an electric feeling of blissful youthfulness. Where had those days gone?

Was I really a 31-year-old being who had forgotten what it was like to love, to be loved?

Wow, I'm suddenly hit by the realization that something is missing from my life, something that I once called my own and I had lost it, or perhaps I had discarded it through non-attention?

Why? Why does any youth make that type of decision? Perhaps, because we so often think there is something better, that the pastures are greener on the other side of the fence.

Who knows for sure how such decisions come about; we just know that they do. Here I was faced with a one-in-a-thousand situation that might allow me to rectify a tragic error; at least that was how it seemed at this second in time.

Remember the movie "*A Moment in Time?*" The atmosphere in the taxi was the same that I experienced while watching that movie (I told you I was a hopeless romantic).

"It was a sad smile just the same"

I glanced in the mirror to view the
fleeting smile once again, and was
rewarded with a reminiscent smile that
had not lost its radiance; instead her smile
had gained a certain wistfulness as well; it
was a sad smile just the same.

She seemed to be recollecting the same
memories that my brain had just accessed;
reaching the same realization that I had
reached, touched by the same breadth of
despair from which I had been touched.

There I go again, seemingly over-
romanticizing the affair. Her smile was
probably nothing more than a smile of
remembrance, not one that recollected
better and more optimistic times; an era of
youth, a sea of turbulence.

Maybe her sad smile had nothing to do
with the sad smile parking itself on my
countenance. Her sad smile could be just
one of general sadness, after all she
herself had opined just a short while ago
the tragic nature of her life.

The fact that she was just a lonely housewife attempting to outrun the lifestyle that had at one time seemed so glamorous and was now so mundane could not possibly play a role in this scenario, could it?

The question that I could have asked (and probably should have) was "are you happy"? But, asking that question is so trite! Who the hell knows if they are happy? That's like asking someone. "are you content, are you satisfied with your life?"

She would have most likely presented her life in a nutshell by stating "what's not to be happy about? Most women would give their eyeteeth to have the things I have; to have access to the money, the wealth, the power, prestige and status that being with my husband affords me".

I wondered to myself; is this how happiness is defined? I know I wasn't happy with some aspects of my current situation in life, but that does not mean I was 'happy' or 'unhappy', right?

Such thinking just meant I needed to make some changes, and change is difficult for some people.

I never seriously thought about asking her that question, but I did wonder if my professorial surmise was close to the target of truth.

Her sad smile seemed to portray the inner conflict that often comes about when an individual has followed a meandering path of life that was not really the path that was wished to travel, but they also did not know how to quit following it; or perhaps they just did not have the inner strength to change the pathway they were traveling.

I grimaced to myself in consternation; was I really that maudlin character who thought that the lady with ownership of everything necessary for a beautifully peaceful and fulfilling life portrayed her conflicted inner soul with a sad, fleeting smile crossing her face.

I think not!

Well, maybe I think not. The romantic in me wanted to push the contending realist encamped in my mind out the back door to allow for the concept of lost true love that had somehow been found and regained in one fell swoop.

All this conjecture and contemplation from her sad smile, I had to humorously smile myself; but my smile was one of vivid recollecting imagination with nary a hint of sadness anywhere close by to be discovered through analytical introspection.

"She said "How are you Harry?"

I heard her whisper something, or at least
I thought she whispered words; perhaps
what influenced the decibel of sound that
resonated through my ear canal was my
own constant introspection into romantic
interludes and imaginations that could not
possibly come to successful fruition.

I asked quickly from my front seat "did
you say something mylady?" and then I
listened intently for her reply.

I heard her voice again, and this time the
rejoinder traveled on love-influenced
soundwaves through the entranceway to
my inner ear, and from there traversed the
short passageway into the cranial cavity
where it blasted upon my brain like a
strong ocean wave against the nearby
cliffs overlooking the Pacific.

She quietly reiterated to me in a slight
quiet question that said it all, "how are
you Harry?"

My brain responded in instant fashion, taking the words before it and then disseminating them to my heart.

Before processing the phrase that was set to penetrate my heart, my brain analyzed the tone, viscosity, veracity and meaning of every syllable contained within the tiny and simple phrase that had presented themselves for analysis.

Like a rocket leaping towards the deep, dark blue sky of a bright Florida sunshine in a fiery display of thundering and encompassing power, my being reveled in those four small words that had been transferred to the vicinity of the feeling romanticized heart by the cool composed brain that had recognized the potential results of the words uttered from the back of the car.

"How are you Harry?" reverberated like a ping pong ball through every pore of my body as a wave of memories threatened to overcome me with no recourse.

If I died this exact second and then, in a million years, researchers found my mummified remains, they would likely be immediately drawn to words "How are you Harry" etched as if in stone upon my bones.

I took a deep composing breath to relieve the pressure on my heart, lungs and soul. The breath worked to calm me, but just barely.

My body had reacted adversely, but at the same time in an exciting manner. I guess memories really do have the capability of affecting us in subtle, and sometimes not so subtle ways.

I was thrilled, overjoyed, that Sue remembered me. I was overcome with feelings of love and passion; not the type of passion that you would find in a bedroom, or an obsessive type of passion, but a passion for something (or someone) beautiful and elegant.

I said, "How are you, Sue?"

I decided to show my cool, my acumen, my control, so I replied with measured calm in my least dramatic voice.

"How are you, Sue?" The words came out not at all like I wanted them to. The words did not convey in any appreciable manner my honest, true feelings of wonderment and discovery. The words seemed to croak out of my chest, and I gulped quickly.

I did not realize just what a momentous experience I was having. I looked in the mirror to gauge her reaction but discovered little there. Her face was in shadow, her body in repose.

It is difficult to describe the exact feelings that emanated from my heart. I wondered to myself if she was feeling the same way. To think that I had Sue in my taxi at that precise moment in time, that I could speak with her if I so desired, that I could tell her the many things that had happened to me since we had parted; it was all so overwhelming to me.

I had not a clue as to where to start. What could I tell her? What could I say to her? I was overcome with a sense of helplessness that I had seldom experienced.

Silence reigned supreme, not just in the front seat of my taxi, where I was still in emotional and mental shock, but from the back seat as well; perhaps due to the same reaction to circumstances that my Sue was experiencing as well.

We both started to talk at the same time.

"How have you been, what have you been up to?"

We questioned each other with a rush, more like an explosion of noise than the rushing sound of verbalization spewing forth from both our throats at the exact same moment. We both laughed self-consciously.

"You first" I allowed graciously. "What would you like to know?"

Sue paused for a second, considering her rejoinder. Then she spoke softly but clearly.

"I want to know how you ended up driving a cab?"

I smiled as I drove.

"Well, I do have to eat" I answered. "I do have to pay rent."

"I realize that," she said impatiently. "But, a taxi driver?"

I squirmed in the front seat, somewhat embarrassed to be discovered in such a low status.

"It pays halfway decently," I assured her. "But, what it really does is gives me time to work on what I really want to do."

"Let me guess," she interjected. "You are still writing poems, songs, and singing."

"Yes." I answered a little more forcefully that what I had desired to. I hurried on before she could notice.

"I am starting to be recognized somewhat" I told her.

"I even have to sign autographs now and again," I chuckled.

"Oh Harry, that's just great!" she replied. "I always knew that you were going to be something special."

"Well, it's not a lot right now, but I have had some talent agents knocking on my door within the last few months. I haven't signed with any of them yet, I want to build up a larger following first before I sign." I paused before continuing on a more truthful path.

"Plus, they have not really offered me much money yet" I explained sheepishly.

"They will!" Sue responded. "I remember your stories and songs quite vividly. You are really good. You were always so good."

I smiled again and looked in the mirror, catching her eye as I did so. I questioned her as we held each other's gaze.

"And, how are you, Sue?" I asked.

"Well, I'm not an actress on Broadway." She grimaced to herself and turned away from my gaze. I turned my attention back to the rain drenched street and my driving.

"What happened?" I asked.

She paused for a second before replying. "The usual. I wasn't quite as good, or quite as beautiful as I thought I was. I started out with a bang, but the entertainment business is brutal. Very cutthroat. I was lucky though."

"In what way," I asked.

"I met David, my husband." She explained hurriedly. "He is very influential in the entertainment business, and he fell for me from the very start. He is very sweet, quite the charmer. With everyone." She added the last phrase almost under her breath.

I waited for a second to see if she was finished.

When it was clear that she did not have anything more to say, I spoke up.

"Are you happy?'

She shook her head in exasperation. "Who is happy?" she retorted. "What is happy?"

Before I could think of a reply, she continued.

"My life is full, I have money. Well, at least David does. I live in a wealthy neighborhood, I have everything I need. Even a loving husband." She snorted in derision at her own comments.

"Ah, Sue." I answered. "It does not sound like it's that bad a life."

"I wanted so much more." She quickly put forth. "I wanted to be known for more than just being my husband's wife!"

We were both silent for a moment contemplating the twists and turns of life's highway and how we had reached the common vehicle in which we now shared a pleasant sojourn.

"Through the too many miles"

A thought crossed my mind as we silently traversed the night roads with the lights from other vehicles flashing across the taxi in which we were ensconced.

"We should have got together before now, we should have kept track of each other, perhaps we should not have ever parted."

I looked in the mirror once again to observe her response before I realized that I had only thought those thoughts, I had not actually spoken them out loud.

"It's been too many miles," I spoke out this thought, not keeping it inside. I could hear her laughter from the back.

"Harry," she said. "I was just thinking the exact same thing."

Before I could reply she said to me, "what do you think about finding a nearby park where we could sit and talk, or maybe walk, for just a little while? I feel like we could do that, what do you think?"

"That's a great idea Sue" I responded. "It just so happens that there is a place just south of here. Although Alamo Square is busy during the day, there's not a lot of traffic there during the night. We should be okay there, especially if this rain stops and we can get out and walk around."

Alamo Square is located on Fulton and Scott Streets and is one of the better (and best maintained) parks in San Francisco. It features plenty of open spaces and observation areas that allow for a great view of downtown San Fran, especially at night.

The park is heavily, but discretely patrolled by San Fran's finest, and the citizens help control its culture as well; they keep out the criminal elements and strive to maintain the park's community environment. It was a perfect place for a tryst. I turned south on Scott Street and headed towards the Square.

We arrived at our destination a few moments later and I pulled into a secluded parking lot.

I pulled the taxi into the first parking lot and slowed to a stop, angling the vehicle into a parking spot away from the nearest bright overhead light.

Turning to her as I switched off the engine, I asked; "What do you think Sue?"

"It's perfect, Harry" she whispered. "It's perfect."

The rain continued to fall, although not nearly as heavily or as noisily as just a few moments ago, perhaps the storm had almost worn itself out. I glanced over the back of the front seat and asked Sue if she would like to sit up front.

"Sure," she chirped, albeit sounding a little nervous. "I don't like having a conversation with the back of your head."

We both laughed self-consciously as she opened the passenger's door and quickly gathered herself into the front seat as I frantically swept the remnants of my earlier meal from the seat and into a small garbage sack I kept for such purposes.

"Good thing I'm not a pig," I quipped as she slid into the seat, slamming the door quickly behind her. She turned to me and smiled her radiant smile.

"You always were meticulous," she laughed. "It made me kind of nervous at times."

"Really?" I asked.

"No Harry, not really." She said. "I was teasing you."

I laughed as well.

"That's good," I said. "I never noticed that you were nervous around me."

She turned to me from her perch and looked me straight in the eye. Now that I could see her face in a clearer fashion, it was easy to recall why I had fallen for her in the first place. The years had been kind to her; she was just as lovely as what I remembered, maybe even more so. Her maturity had added to her loveliness. Her beauty took my breath away.

Sue reached out with her hand and touched my arm.

Her touch sent an electric current soaring through my body; like a light circuit being completed, my response was to feel infused.

"It's been too long Harry," she remarked. "I have thought about you a lot."

"Oh Sue," I replied. "I had forgotten just what a beautiful person you are."

She smiled somewhat whimsically, and pulled her hand away from arm. My entire being regretted not having the contact after she broke it; the resulting feeling was as if a source of energy had been withdrawn from contact.

"And the two little smiles"

We sat there quietly as the rain drummed on the roof of the taxi over our heads. I looked in her eyes, as she looked in mine.

Finally, a smile suddenly appeared on her face, and I had to smile in return. The two little smiles mirrored our thoughts, and I could see in an instant that Sue was the exact same person that I had once knew, loved and cherished. With her smile, I knew without a doubt that she was feeling the same way. My heart soared with exultation.

"Tell me something Sue," I said as I gazed intently into her eyes. "Why did we part? What in the world were we thinking?"

Sue emitted a small laugh. "Seriously? Harry? Don't you remember?"

I drew back, taken aback.

"No." I answered with alacrity. "What I remember is that I loved you unlike any other soul I have ever met."

"Humph," she halfway grunted. "If you had stuck around, I would have married you in a heartbeat. But," she paused "you were too wild, too uncontrollable, too destined for greatness!"

"Yeah right," I answered with derision. "I'm a taxi cab driver, not a very great position in life."

Sue reached out to touch me again. "You will achieve greatness Harry, I know it, I believe it, I've always thought so."

I basked in her belief for just a second.

"Thank you, Sue," I replied. "That means a lot to me."

We both smiled at each other into the darkness of the front seat of the cab once again. The smiles were little smiles, but smiles none the less.

Seeing her here, having her so close by, provided a missing ingredient in my life; the support of a woman who believed in me. I had forsaken that aspect of my life, I had erased any hope of having that as part of me.

"I still remember you"

I reached out and took Sue's hand into my own, softly caressing her palm with the thumb of my right hand.

"I remember when this used to drive you nuts," I invoked softly as I continued the slight brushing action.

I gazed into her eyes and saw my reflection within them; I reveled within that reflection and remembered how the intensity contained within her return gaze had captivated me from the first moment, the first second, the first millisecond of time I was with her.

I knew from that very start that we were meant to be, that we would be a pair, a couple, we would be together forever. I remembered that, and I remembered so much more.

As I continued to tease her palm, she relaxed into her seat with a small sigh of contentment.

"I haven't had anyone do that in so long," she whispered.

We both sat in silence for a few moments, slowly relaxing while thinking our own thoughts.

I wondered if the thoughts rolling through her head were the same rumbling through mine, or at least that they were along the same vein. I kept her hand in mine, turning in my seat to face her more fully head on.

"Do you remember the very first time we went out? I took you to that empty theater in Newark, and put on a one-man show for you."

Sue laughed out loud. "That's right," she said. "We snuck in the back, and had the entire place to ourselves. I remember thinking, well this is a first."

"I know, I could not afford to take you anywhere that would have cost me more than $10 and I also wanted to impress you with my wit and charm."

"You certainly did that. I especially liked the original Shakespearean poem that you wrote just for me."

"I still have the copy you made me, in fact, I had the poem framed and it is sitting on my bureau."

"Wow," I replied. "That's pretty impressive. What does your husband say about that?"

"He's okay with it. He's not the jealous type, plus he does his thing and I do mine."

"Really? I can't imagine that. I would never let you out of my sight, if you were my wife."

Sue left forth a burst of laughter.

"Oh Harry, you haven't changed one little bit." She laughed again. "That's what I always liked about you, Harry. You were so gallant."

"That was not gallantry," I quickly retorted. "That was love."

"Yeah, puppy love." She said, then she quickly changed the subject, steering our thoughts away from a place she did not wish to go.

"Another thing I remember about you Harry was that you were never at a loss for new ideas, you were not afraid to try something new."

"In fact," she continued before I could intervene, "you pretty much owned the idea of trying new things."

"Yep, I did" I agreed. "And what I remember was that you were right there with me every step of the way."

"We made quite a pair back then, didn't we, Harry?" She reminisced.

The silence following her question was a comfortable one that filled the cab with a sense of fond recollections.

"It was somewhere in a fairy tale"

"I was so happy back then, it was like a fairy tale come true." She whispered the words into the silence. "You were my prince, and you made everything alright in my life."

"And you were my Queen," I quickly reminded her. "My only wish was to give you a kingdom."

"It's too bad that we had to grow up and live in reality," she said.

"Yeah, look at me now," I exclaimed throwing my arms wide, "I'm driving a yellow chariot for Mylady."

"Why thank Sir Knight," Sue replied, jumping right into the game. "I'm sure the King will be impressed."

"Hmmmm," I continued to playact. "I'm pretty sure the evil Sorcerer has put him under a spell. He only wishes to keep you locked in your tower, away from the influences of a poor pauper such as myself."

"I guess you will have to rescue me then."

We both fell silent as the double importance of our words encroached upon our real lives.

Sue slowly pulled her hand away. "Perhaps, we should head home. The King will likely be wondering the whereabouts of his Queen." She told me ruefully.

"Is that what you wish?" I asked. "Look, I turned the meter off! Can we talk just a few moments more?"

Sue squeezed my hand. "Are you sure that's all you want to do?"

"Of course, that's not all I wish to do," I retorted. "Now that I found you again, I would love to sweep you off your feet, take you into my arms, toss you on the back of my trusty white steed, and ride off into the sunset. But, you're married, I'm poor, and all I have in life right now are my songs and trying to make it big."

Sue looked me in the eye. "You never understood that about me, did you Harry?"

"Understood what?"

"I wasn't joking a short while ago when I told you that you were my Prince, I always believed in you, I was always more than willing to help you achieve greatness."

"I understood that part of it Sue, but, I also understood that I wanted to give you more than a life filled with poverty and dreaming. I wanted to build you a castle, and give you all the finer things that life has to offer."

She looked me in the eye, searching for something that I'm not sure was there.

"I know you did Harry, but it's not the end rewards that I was interested in, it was the journey that I wished to travel with you, I wanted to share your life, your joys, your pain, your sorrows. You never did understand that, did you?"

"I guess not," I said after a bit of reflection. "In my defense, I was always so poor when I was growing up, that material items meant a lot to me. I was tired of being poor and I viewed myself in terms of what I could offer a woman materially. That was a mistake wasn't it?"

"Yes, Harry, it was."

We both sat back and contemplated the mistakes we had made. It was a perfect example of the follies of youth when our communication skills are not at their highest levels; come to think of it, I know plenty of people who lack those skills even though they are already adults.

I attempted to lighten the somber mood we had created between ourselves in the front seat of my taxi. "I did not have much practice at being a prince, but I sure did my best with what I had."

"I know, Harry. I never blamed you for what happened between us, I blamed the circumstances."

She paused for a second and then quietly continued, so much so that I barely heard her last words. "It seemed too much like a fairy tale, and I guess it was."

"I used to take her home in my car"

We both sat silent, contemplating the distant past, an unknown future, and the here and now. Shaking her golden tresses in a similar manner to a massive lion's mane, she broke the contemplative mood in resounding fashion.

Turning to me, she remarked, "the front seat of this vehicle is nothing like the one that we used to share."

I laughed at the memory. "Nah," I said. "Remember how I used to take you home in my car, and we would wonder if it would actually make it there."

"That isn't what I remember about the car," Sue said with a laugh. "But, you are right, that conveyance was definitely a piece of crap."

"Hey," I protested. "It was the best I could do with the little bit that I earned cleaning dishes at Cheesecake Factory."

"Do you remember the duct tape that we used on the seat to prevent me from falling into the cracks?" Sue laughed.

"We spent almost an entire afternoon trying to patch those seats."

"What I remember was how ugly that automobile was," I grimaced. "I was so embarrassed to be driving it."

"I bet you were the only boy in our high school that drove a puke-yellow Dodge with duct tape holding the seats together." Her voice trilled in a pleasing manner as she recalled the pleasant times we had shared in our youth.

"Well, again, I was just happy that I was able to offer you rides, it gave me time to be with you; and that was worth far more than anything else I could ever think of."

I looked at Sue before adding; "I may have had the ugliest car, but I also had the prettiest girl in the entire school."

"Thank you, Harry. You make me feel brand new."

I showed her my hands, "Do you recall how I was always worried about having to fix that car? How I worried that it might ruin my guitar-playing capabilities?"

"Yeah," Sue replied. "Are you still that way?"

"Yep, yep, yep." I quipped. "Don't even wish to get my hands dirty."

"Well, the one thing that I was always impressed with," Sue grinned, "was your guitar-playing fingers!"

"Sue! Wow! I can't believe you just said that" I joked. We laughed at each other.

"We learned about love in the back of a Dodge"

"Speaking of which," I transitioned. "Do you remember the back seat of that car? We had some very good times back there."

"Yeah," she said dryly. "You took my virginity in that back seat."

"You also took mine," I replied. "And, I never once regretted it."

"Neither did I, Harry. You were quite a special person back in the day."

"What do you mean, back in the day?" I teasingly retorted. "I'm still a special person, just ask my mom, she tells me I'm '*special*' all the time."

"I'll bet she does," answered Sue. "I always liked your mother, how is she?"

"She's as feisty as ever," I answered.

"And your dad?"

"Same ole, same old," I replied.

"Surprisingly enough, the last time I saw them, which was only about a month ago, they asked about you."

"Really?" She acted surprised. "What did they say?"

"Just wondered if I had heard from you." I reached across and took her hand in mine once again. "You were quite a hit with my parents."

"Oh, and I wasn't a hit with you?" she asked with a mischievous grin.

"You know you were mylady! And, it wasn't just making love to you in the back seat either. Although, that was definitely part of it!"

"Yeah that was mighty nice." She shook her head ruefully. "They were very good times, Harry." She looked up at me with seriousness in her eyes before she asked, "Do you regret any of it?"

"How could I regret those times? Seriously! The only thing I regret is the fact that I let you get away."

"The lesson hadn't gone too far"

We were both taken aback by the passion in my voice as I answered her. I was surprised that I felt so strongly, that I still felt so much love.

Was it love that I was feeling? I'm not sure, all I know for sure is that my current feelings were just as strong and overwhelming as they were way back in the day when Sue and I were a young couple in love.

"It's fine," I shrugged. "This car has seen a lot worse, that's for sure." I turned my head to study the park and to hide the emotion in my eyes.

How could I still feel love for this beautiful woman when I had not seen her in over 15 years? How could the attraction still be so strong? We had lived separate lives, we had tread different paths. Had I not learned a single, solitary thing about the love that I discovered in the back of that Dodge?

I could tell that Sue was surprised as well, and perhaps a little upset with me. Her face reflected the emotions conflicting within her; I recognized those clashing thoughts because the same ones were blasting their way around my brain, filling my soul with emotions I had not felt in years.

I was now in my early thirties, and I asked myself; what the hell? Was I that big a dufus that I still had not learned the lessons of love?

Of course, it could be that love lessons are the hardest, the most difficult to come to terms with, and perhaps neither one of us had really learned that lesson as of yet.

Here I was waxing philosophic in the front seat of a taxi. How ironic; thinking of the lessons of a backseat whilst stuck in the front.

Not that Sue and I were thinking about this specific backseat, but the concept was there for the plucking; we had shared the most intimate of times in the back seat of my Dodge, and those times were difficult to forget, even if our thoughts were so dissonant 15 years later.

I drew a deep, comforting breath to calm my racing heart and emotions.

"What are you thinking, Harry" Sue asked me quietly.

I paused for a second or two before replying.

"I truly don't know what I am thinking Sue. I'm a true romantic, and ultimately I believe that fate has something in store for each of us."

"Does fate mean that you and I were supposed to go fifteen years without seeing each other, does it mean that you and I will go another fifteen years, and then another fifteen years after that, before seeing each other? I don't know."

"I don't know enough about love, about sharing my life, about allocating my experiences with someone except on a casual basis, and I could never think of you as anything but casual."

I heaved a sigh as I finished, exhausted with the effort to explain myself, my feelings, when I did not recognize those feelings with any semblance of sanity.

"Wow, Harry. You really have some issues." She laughed at my consternation. "I'm teasing you, don't you know that?"

"Yeah, I know. But, do you understand what I am trying to say? What I am trying to convey to you? I'm trying to be more than just a romantic songwriter, I want to make sense, I want comprehension, and I'm not sure that I am either expressing it or understanding it the way I wish to, or the way I wish you would, or could."

Sue squeezed my hand and smiled.

"Harry don't take yourself so serious, it does not become you. What we had back in those days was special, there is no denying that fact."

She took her hand and turned my face towards her, forcing me to focus on her face.

"It is destiny that we met here in San Francisco, on this rainy night, in your cab. Sometimes fate pulls funny tricks on us to give us a kickstart in a direction that we might not have gone without fortune's intervention."

"Just think," Sue continued. "You could end up writing a top-ten song from this encounter. You could call it "Sue," or "Rainy Night in Frisco," or even "Taxi".

I smiled at the thought and added a phrase to what I already had for the song, "the lesson had not gone too far."

My song was coming to fruition and selfishly I thought to myself that I might just end up with an even more comprehensive understanding of love, at least I hoped so.

Would such an understanding help me become an even better songwriter, a more empathetic man? Was that what fate was attempting to show me? Was that the reason Sue was in the front seat of my taxi?

Talk about not learning the lessons of love, I was the perfect description.

I looked Sue in the eye and told her, "Sue, this may not mean much now, but I believe that there was a reason we were together a long time ago, and I believe there is a reason we met tonight."

Sue smiled her radiant smile. "Harry, there is always rhyme and reason to everything that happens. We are slated to learn from every event that takes place in our lives, including young puppy love."

"Do you really think that is what it was?" I questioned her searchingly.

"Who knows? I haven't learned that lesson yet."

That's the problem I thought to myself, neither have I. I commiserated with her with a faint smile.

"You see, she was gonna be an actress"

I finally just shrugged my shoulders and shook my head, breaking the spell that had surrounded us in the confined spaces of the front seat of the taxi.

"Tell me Sue," I said with a quick grin. "What happened to the idea of you becoming an actress? You certainly still have the looks for it!"

She smiled at the compliment and then turned serious as she contemplated her reply and the reasons for not achieving the goals and objectives that we often set for ourselves when we are young and naïve.

Sue informed me in our very first conversation together that her wildest dream, her one goal, her most sincere objective was to become an actress; not the type of actress that is as well-known or famous as someone like Marilyn Monroe (even though Sue had the looks for it) but a serious, well-respected lady of film and entertainment.

I believe, strike that…I know! I know that one of the reasons Sue and I had parted was that we allowed our dreams to come between us, we allowed our own personal goals and objectives to take precedence over our shared interests and desires.

Was that a foolish action on our part? I don't know, I haven't achieved what I set out to achieve, and it seems like Sue was currently in the same situation as me.

Perhaps we are far too selfish when we are young; despite the fervent, hot, discovery nature of our sexual frolicking that had us believing that we were meant to be together forever, we still allowed our dreams of a future outside the realms of "puppy love" to influence us even more than the puppy love itself. It was an interesting paradigm.

You see, she wanted to be an actress. I can understand that, and, in fact, I understand it even now.

She wanted to chase her dreams, I did not wish to hold her back; after all, I had dreams of my own; goals and objectives, hopes, and desires. I believe I loved her, and that we would be happy together, but just like her, I was unwilling to take the chance that it would not work out between us.

Looking around our hometown, it's understandable. So many of the young people who got married right out of high school (and in some cases before graduating high school) were still stuck in the same old town, some with a kid or two (or three or four), some in trailer park homes, many of them drinkers, gamblers and worse. Is it any wonder whatsoever that Sue wanted out of that mantra?

I certainly was not the one to hold her back; I too had a yearning, a desire, hopes and dreams that would compel me to leave our hometown behind in a quick cloud of dust.

"I was going to learn to fly"

While Sue was dreaming of becoming an actress, I was going to learn to fly; not just be a pilot to be a pilot, not be a pilot because they can earn a good living; I wished to learn to fly because it would give me the proper perspective on life itself.

Back then, my youthful exuberance and lack of real-world experience bolstered my belief that flying would provide me with a comprehensive knowledge and understanding that I would be unable to attain in any other manner, or through any other means.

Isn't that the essence of life; our childhood dreams, our youthful desires, sharing them, dreaming them, they seem so real, so attainable when we are young, but then we grow old and look at where, and how, we end up driving taxi's.

Here we are; Sue and I, in a dingy, yellow taxicab parked at Alamo Square in downtown San Francisco in the rain.

How short time seems to be; how quickly time flies by, oftentimes leaving our hopes, our dreams, our unfulfilled aspirations behind us in another life.

I look across the seat and see an angel; a woman in a damp dress who had such an influence in a previous life, that I had taken off from my small-town roots to travel half-way across the vaunted plains and mountains of America because I believed I could learn to fly. How ironic the circumstances, how simple life turns out to be, if we can but see it in its simple glory.

One might even be able to say that the effort to spread one's wings, the attempt to justify one's existence, the simple act of pushing forward towards our ultimate goal, provides all the impetus necessary for achieving the dreams of our youth. But, have we really attained anything at all, if we still aren't where we expected to be?

I did not realize that I had been waxing eloquent until Sue interrupted me.

"Harry," she said. "You are going off on one of your tangents again."

I looked at her in amazement.

"Ah crap!" I said convincingly. "You always did bring out the philosopher from deep within me."

She laughed in a pleasant manner.

"Harry," she said, "that was philosophizing at its very best. One of the things that I always loved about you was that you were oftentimes on a different plane than the rest of humanity. That's how I know that you will achieve greatness, it's rooted within you."

"When you told me that you were going to learn to fly, I never once believed that it meant you were going to be a pilot; I knew that it meant you would reach heights that the rest of humanity could only dream of."

I smiled at her for her words of wisdom. Even years later, she knew exactly what to say to me.

"She took off to find the footlights"

After listening to, and absorbing her words, I turned the tables on her with my next question.

"Okay Sue, do you remember how we parted? I sure do!"

"Yes," she answered slowly. "It was not one of my better moments."

"I know!" I replied emphatically. "One day you are there, and the very next day you are gone. You didn't really even say goodbye to me, you just left."

"That's because you would have convinced me to stay," she retorted. "Besides, it was best for both of us."

"Yeah." I said sardonically. "I was heart-broken for years."

"Oh Harry, you were not. I know for a fact that you struck out on your own, shortly after I left there."

"That's because I had to! You left me no choice, I didn't even know where you went."

We both were breathing hard with the memories of our parting years ago. I took a deep breath and settled my nerves. I laid a tremulous hand on her golden tresses, brushing them back from her face.

"I'm sorry Sue," I told her. "I have no right whatsoever to be upset with you. I knew deep within my heart that you were pursuing your dream, and if you wish to know the truth, when you left to pursue your own ambitions, it actually provided me with the impetus to pursue my own."

"Really?" Sue questioned me.

"Yes," I replied. "I would have never have left New Jersey if you were still there to cling to. You were my rock, my anchor, my key to a comfortable life, and with you gone, I knew that I had to face life on my own, I had to achieve my goals and aspirations using just my own wits, skills and knowledge."

"You can see how that turned out," I told her expansively.

Sue laughed at my sense of humor. "Harry, you will achieve the greatness that you so deserve. Sometimes we as individuals have to experience the very doldrums of life in order to move forward into glory. If that were not true, then how could you take your experiences and not use them for your songs, your poems and your stories. You had to experience the bad times to effectively write about them. Am I right?"

I reflected on her words before slowly answering her.

"I think you are. In fact, you are right!"

It was an epiphany for me. I realized at that exact moment that she clearly understood and could explain to me the way that life works.

Because she left me in Newark, without the support that I so desperately clung to, she had forced me to accept the challenges of a life that would provide me with stories to be told both through song and rhyme. Her very act of leaving forced me to accept the challenge!

"And I took off to find the sky"

Sue had left Newark without a word to me. Actually; that's not true. She had told me in no uncertain terms that she was ready to move on, to pursue her dream, but I had not believed her. I could not believe her; I knew she loved me, and that our love would keep us together forever.

Little did I know, that she loved me so much, she would set me free. In retrospect, it was exactly what I needed.

I turned to Sue in the front seat of my taxi and said quite simply "Thank you Sue. You always loved me, didn't you?"

"Yes, Harry, I did."

I sat back in the driver's seat and contemplated the night's events. It is amazing to me that we can oftentimes forget to see the world for what it is, instead we view the world for what we think it should be; and that's just as true when we are older and wiser as it is when we are younger and dumber.

I realized now, that what Sue had wanted for me was that I go forth and spread my wings; learn to fly, experience life, learn from it, and then use that knowledge and wisdom to further develop as a human, as a man, as an individual, as a songwriter, as a singer, as an entertainer.

She must have known, even then, that I would need a push out the door to get me started. At the time, I did not realize what was taking place. In fact, it did not even dawn on my imagination until this night in San Francisco in the front seat of my taxi, with Sue, as the rain pounded down upon the roof over our heads.

Now, here we were together, and the truth hung between us like a scepter in the night, ready to either cut the ties between us, or bless us with it's strength. I hoped for the latter, rather than the former.

"I guess you now understand why I had to leave you, right Harry?"

"Yes, Sue. I do now. It sure did hurt a lot back then though."

"I figured that it would, but, I did not know what else to do. You were so focused on our future together, it drove me nuts."

"I loved you completely, or so I thought anyway." I chuckled quietly to myself, but Sue still heard me.

"It's not funny. It was a very tough choice. The only reason why I chose the way I did was because I loved you so much. I knew that if we had stayed together, you would have ended up hating me."

"Wait, wait, wait" I exclaimed. "I would have never hated you."

"Well, maybe hate is not the right word, but you would have definitely never forgiven me, and you may have even grown to despise me. I couldn't take that chance, Harry. I loved you too much!"

It hit me like a ton of bricks; she was right. If we had married, my artistic endeavors would have been constrained forever.

My ambition would have withered away like a grape vine during the winter; still alive, still with a root that could blossom, grow and sustain fruit, but with a huge likelihood of facing too many icy storms to survive.

My heart suddenly filled with a precious love and understanding of what she had done for me.

I drew her hand to my lips and lightly brushed them against her digits.

"Thank you, Sue," I breathed. "You are truly a remarkable individual. Your husband is a lucky man."

"Well, I sure wish he thought that," she remarked with an underlying current of derision emanating from her throat. Before I could make any remark, she continued; "I just wanted you to learn to fly."

The front seat of the cab was quiet both on the passenger side and on the driver's side. I guess we both were remembering how our parting came to pass; or at least I was remembering; I could only assume that Sue was as well based upon her non-responsiveness and the manner on which she was looking at me.

It was not a pleasant thought for me; I remembered being devastated when she left, moping around for days, feeling like a lost little puppy without a home.

Sue had warned me that she was leaving, but I did not believe she really would. There were no cell phones at that time, so it wasn't like the instant communication that we have nowadays, she did not text me and say "yo, I'm out of here," instead she told me in person that the next time I came to see her, she would not be there.

I knew in my heart that she was really leaving, but I had hoped against hope that it would not be true, that she would change her mind, that she would admit that our love was too strong to discard. Alas; it was not to be.

On that fateful day, I drove to her house located on the outskirts of town.
Once I reached there, I parked my Dodge in the driveway and walked up to her front door.

Normally, she would have seen me coming and met me at the door, that day the only greeting I received was from Muttly, her family's black and white half-breed dog that hung out on her front porch. Reaching down, I scratched the dog behind his ears in a way that I knew he liked.

"What's up Muttly?" I asked him rhetorically. "Where's Sue?"

He looked up at me with brown sad eyes, as if he knew exactly what I was asking and understood that the answer would not make me a happy camper.

Sue's mother appeared holding a dish towel in her hand; she opened the front door to speak with me.

"Hi Harry," she exclaimed. "What are you doing here?"

"Uhmmm," I stammered. "I thought I might see if Sue changed her mind?"

"Oh, Harry. She did not. I'm so sorry, did you really think she would?"

"No." I answered. "But, a guy can hope, right?"

I tried to put a brave face on the situation, but I think her mom knew what it was that I was really feeling. She offered me some lemonade, but I was not in the mood.

"She really left then?" I queried.

"Yes, Harry she did." Her mom looked at me with sadness in her eyes, I just turned and walked away. I never saw her mother again, and until tonight I thought I never would see Sue again as well.

Fate and fortune had intervened to provide me with one more chance to make things right.

Shortly after discovering that Sue had taken the steps necessary to achieve her dream, and long before I wanted to, I left New Jersey as well.

I packed my meager belongings into the Dodge, gave my mother a hug, shook my dad's hand, got in my vehicle, and off I went. My destination was Colorado; there I would immerse myself in the mountainous environment, and enroll in flight school.

Sue had promised to keep in contact from California, and I figured that living only three states from her, instead of across the entire country, it would mean that we would be much more likely to continue our romance; like I mentioned earlier, I am a definite romantic.

Little did I realize how difficult it would be to maintain a romance from 1500 miles away; especially when we both were striving so hard to achieve our dreams.

Sue and I had continued our correspondence, and maintained our faithfulness to each other for approximately six months before I met another girl who took my eye.

By that time, letters from Sue were few and far between, and I was pretty sure she had found someone new as well. It was much simpler to move on than it was to maintain a long-distance relationship, and probably much better for us both.

Now, here she was sitting in the front-seat of my taxi, looking and smelling exactly as I remembered her. What was I supposed to do now?

"Whoa, I've got something inside me"

Suddenly, it hit me; here I was with the opportunity to rectify a past wrong and while doing so perhaps recover from the effects of the very scenario that I was attempting to rectify.

In that second of time, I realized that I could take action that would change the course of my life, if I allowed it to.

I hesitated before speaking out; questioning my motivation, was this what I really wanted? Was it truly fate that Sue was here in my taxi cab with me that night? If it was destiny, was I supposed to take action that would bring us back together? These questions and more, jumbled in my mind and stayed my words and my desires.

Before I could accept the responsibility of my chosen pathway, I had to ensure that the pathway was the one that I truly desired. Hence, my hesitation to tell Sue exactly what I was contemplating.

Before I could say anything to her, she spoke up.

"It's alright Harry" she said. "I know what you have inside you. You always were the one person in my life that I knew as well as I knew myself. Please don't be conflicted, we will both be fine."

I looked at Sue in amazement. She was right, as usual. She knew my most intimate thoughts, it was like she and I were one person, her knowing my thoughts, and my knowing hers.

That's what I missed the most about Sue; it had been years and years since we had seen each other, been together, shared our bodies and our hearts, yet still she could look at the man inside me and touch him while using no physical means whatsoever. Perhaps together we shared what most people would never know; true love.

The thought of true love actually made me sad, not only me that is; but also the man inside me.

I can't even explain it in words that make complete sense; how do you go about explaining something inside you that's unexplainable?

Similar to the story of the seven blind men and the elephant; each one of them felt a different part of the elephant and when asked to describe the animal, could only do so based upon the part of the elephant that each individual felt. On described the elephant as a hose, the other a rope, the third as a tree stump, and on and on. Each one gave a unique and quite different description. That would be me trying to describe the animal inside me; it was different things on different days and different times. Sue may be the only person I know that could describe the man inside me in a complete and comprehensive manner.

I knew the man was there, lurking sometimes, boldly asserting itself at other times, as it was seeking to do right now, in my taxi, with Sue. I had to rein it in, keep it under control, not allow it to manifest itself in any way at all. I looked at Sue and smiled faintly.

"I've missed you Sue," I said.

She smiled in response. "You will never know Harry how much I regret walking away from you. Never."

She placed her hand on my chest over my heart and kept it there.

"There is something inside you Harry that makes you a wonderful person."

"To drive a princess blind"

"I don't know what it is," she said as she kept her hand on my chest.

I could feel my heart beating and knew that she could as well. "It's my heart," I told her in a half-joking manner.

She withdrew her hand in disappointment.

"No, Harry that's not what I was referring to. You are a special person, and we both know it. I used to be blind about it, but over the years I've come to realize just how special you really are."

"Wow." I replied. "I wish you had told me that a long, long time ago."

"I couldn't back then, Harry. I was blind to it."

I sat back from her, in amazement. "So, you left me way back when because you thought I was a special person? That doesn't make much sense to me."

She hesitated before replying. "Yes, I knew you were special, I did not know how special, but it was there."

"I knew that if you continued on with me, that if you did not spread your wings and fly, that you would never reach your fullest potential, and there was the possibility that you would forever hold that against me."

"Humph. That's interesting," I replied. "You act like you were an anchor around my neck, but the way I saw it was that you were the wind beneath my wings."

"Now you sound like Bette Midler," she laughed.

"You were a sweetheart!" I protested. I was in love with you, I saw a future with you."

"What kind of future Harry? Seriously, what kind of future would we have had?"

"Here is what would have happened," she told me. "We would have been married, had kids, you would have had to find a job, we would have gotten all caught up in the circle of life. Your dreams would have been smashed."

She took a deep breath but before I could respond to her, she continued. "I did not want to be the reason for your dashed dreams. I was blind with reason."

"I wish you would have told me this before you left. We could have worked something out."

"No, we could not have. It wouldn't have worked."

"Well, it sure did not work out anyway, right? Are you happy? Have I achieved my dreams? I think the answer to both of those questions is a resounding no. Am I wrong? I'm driving a taxi for hell's sake." I answered my own questions in a deprecating manner.

Sue was silent for a moment as we both contemplated our words.

"You made me blind, Harry. I saw that special something inside you, and knew you were destined for far greater things than marriage and family."

"What could be more important?" I asked her. "Nothing is more important than family."

"You know what, Harry? You just might be right. But, that's all in the past now. We can't change the past."

"There's a wild man, wizard Hidden inside me, illuminating my mind"

I thought hard about what Sue had just told me. She had recognized something special inside me; what is really strange about her observation was that I grew up believing that there was something inside me, a sort of wizard that was there to assist me throughout my life.

My wizard (who I named Merlin – I know that name is trite!) helped me to understand a lot of things, events, happenings, and experiences that have affected me throughout my life, sometimes on a daily basis.

What was remarkable about my Merlin, was that I had never told anyone else, not even Sue, about him. No one knew about Merlin, except me. Yet, Sue had just informed me that she had figured out my wizard and knew there was something inside me special. Wow! I was just floored.

Imagine if you can, your deepest secret, your firmest belief, something that you have never told anyone.

Now imagine finding out from someone you haven't seen in years, that they knew your secret the entire time. If you can do that, you'll know the feeling I was experiencing right then.

The scary part about Sue knowing my wizard, was that while 90% of the time my wizard was there to help me, and his services had been very beneficial in the past, he was also a mad man at times, instead of illuminating my mind, he goaded me into accepting risks that I should not accept, oftentimes acting obsessive, and more than often being a very possessive person.

I realize that I am describing myself, because after all, even the devils within us are still under our control. Sometimes, it's just difficult to control our angels, especially when they wish to act like devils instead.

One good thing about the wizard inside me, my devil, my angel, is that whichever role he was playing, he constantly strove to illuminate my mind.

Because he (I always considered him a guy) was both devil and angel, he was able to present me from within the good side, and the bad side, of every situation. He illuminated my mind with the thoughts, desires and analysis of what we could accomplish together. Of course, some of hisl ideas were purely evil, whilst other thoughts were just heavenly.

Maybe it's the same way with everyone; every individual has a certain character within them that is both evil and good; a character that can supply enough good ideals to save the human race, and enough bad ideals to sink an entire boat of Christians.

So, which one do we listen to? Which side of the character deep within us is the one that influences our pathway, our actions, our choices more than the other?

How do we decide which wizard will
provide more long-term influences in our
short-term lives?

It was an interesting conundrum for sure,
one that I would be addressing through
thought and deed for the remainder of my
life.

The best part about the realization that
Sue had discovered the animal within me,
had known all along that it was there, was
the acknowledgement that I was no longer
alone as the only person on the planet
with a wizard inside them illuminating
their lives, and their minds.

*"Oh, I've got something inside me
Not what my life's about"*

What I realized right then was that we are all special people, that we all make sacrifices for others, that we all choose our own paths through life, every individual is constantly seeking to determine his or her own path, their own fate, their own adventures and misadventures.

Some of us, probably many of us, contemplate that wizard inside us to more fully determine what direction we should take, but that's not what my life's about.

My life is about chronicling my thoughts, words, deeds and the very adventures and misadventures that we all experience.

I have often thought that I had a higher pathway, that I lived on a higher plane than many of those who I have met, those with whom I have experienced life.

I've considered my songwriting as similar to a calling from the big man in the sky; that by writing and singing about life and its joys and sorrows, I could bring joy to my listeners, and some respite to the every day travails and hardships that every single human endures.

I turned to Sue and asked her, "Do you think I'm a good person?"

"I don't think you are a good person, Harry. I know you are a good person. You are probably one of the best people that I have ever known – or ever will know."

"Thank you, Sue," I answered her fervently. "You don't know how much that means to me."

Before I continued, I thought about my next words very carefully.

"You are the only person that knows what's inside me Sue. That makes you even more special than me. But, that little man inside me, is not what my life's about."

"Cause I've been letting my outside tide me"

I tried to explain to her the feelings that were doing their best to overcome me at that specific moment.

"I think that meeting you here this way, picking you up in my taxi tonight, is not due to fate, but could be due to a much higher force than that. I have been sliding along in this life for so long; doing my best to ignore the life force within me. I'm still writing my songs, but not with the fervor that they desired, or needed. Maybe that's why I'm still here in San Francisco driving a taxi for tips. I've been letting my outside tide me, over my inside."

Sue quietly contemplated me and thought about what I had just told her. She took a deep breath and then replied to me.

"Well, Harry, maybe it wasn't fate that brought us together, but it sounds like it could be the much-needed event that propels you forward into the future; if you choose to allow it to. What do you think?" she asked.

When I did not answer right away, she asked, "Do you think you could allow our meeting to overcome whatever it is that is holding you back from achieving the greatness that is within you?"

"I don't know, Sue" I answered truthfully. "It seems like there has always been something holding me back, and I never could figure out what it was."

"Well now you can take what has happened here in this taxi tonight and use it, if you will, in a manner that will be conducive to a successful and brilliant songwriting and singing career; to achieve the greatness that we both know is within you. You will no longer find it necessary to "let your outside tide you.""

A sudden feeling of warmth and compassion filled my breast with love and desire; a feeling that led me to believe that I really could do the things that Sue was espousing; I really could be the singer/songwriter to captivate the hearts and souls of millions of fans.

The song that had been filtering through my creative processes continued to grow, continued to flesh itself out.

In fact, as I was sitting there contemplating the vagaries of life, a title for the song popped into my head; I would call it "Taxi".

Could this be the song that would start me on the right pathway? Could I have passed into a new direction that would bring me the success, the fame, the glory that I have always craved and desired? I fervently hoped so.

I could already discern a difference between my pre-Taxi life, and my current attitude and capabilities. I was no longer letting my outside tide me.

"Over 'till my time, runs out"

I just hoped it wasn't too late; I had spent my entire adult life (and most of my youth) not listening wholeheartedly to my inner being, and plowing ahead on a street that was as untraveled as a dead-end alley in a dying ghetto.

I hoped I had not waited too long; that my time would not run out before I could accomplish the success that I was destined for, at least according to Sue and now according to my inner self.

This night in the taxi had sure turned out a lot differently than I had imagined earlier in the evening. Never in my wildest dreams had I thought that what was taking place, would take place.

"You have helped me so much tonight," I whispered to Sue. "I'm hoping that it makes a difference."

"You still have time, Harry. Life hasn't past you by yet." She reached out and took my hand once again.

"You need to grasp life by the hand and pull it along with you, taking the good from it, and learning from the bad."

"I've learned so much tonight," I told her. "The main thing that I have learned is that you are a tremendous individual. You are exactly what I have needed in my life. Especially right now."

Sue pulled back a little from me, leaning against the passenger's door. She looked at me intently.

"Harry," she began, but before she could continue, I held my finger up to her lips.

"Shhh," I shushed. "Don't say it, I already know."

Sue smiled sadly. "I am sorry. I feel the same as you. But, there is nothing that I can do. I'm married, and I'm not willing to do anything at all to jeopardize that marriage, even if it is a sham. There is something else you need to know as well."

Here I had been thinking that I was handling life just fine, but I was only living on the outside, not the inside.

I hoped to myself that I was not too late; that I was not at a point where my time had run out, at least I sincerely hoped that was true. I wondered to myself why it took a wonderful lady from my past to see where I was in my present.

I find it very intriguing that momentous events can happen in our lives at precisely the time when they are so desperately needed to take place.

I looked at Sue and imagined the life that we would have had together, was she correct in her thinking? Had I been living the outside life for so long, that I was unable to see the inside life?

I shifted gears from within and wondered why she was so sorry. It would be one thing if she was happy with her life but she did not seem to be so. Were there other circumstances of which I was unaware? That's an interesting thought.

I turned my attention to Sue to determine those circumstances, of which I was totally unaware.

Before I forged ahead into an area that I might regret going, I contemplated her eyes and her countenance one more time.

"Baby's so high that she's skying"

"What's really up with your life Sue?" I asked as I searched her eyes for the truth. "What's going on?"

Sue again pulled away from me, crossing her arms in front of her as she tried to hug herself.

I waited patiently for her response; I realized that something important was going to be said, and I wanted to give it my complete attention. The silence continued for another moment.

Finally, she broke the silence.

"Harry, I'm sick, and I may not get better. I'm on all kinds of medicines to help, but so far, they haven't really worked. Half the time I feel like I'm as high as a kite. Maybe that's why I'm not happy; my husband looks at it as more of a burden for him, than it is for me."

I was shocked! I was flabbergasted. I had no idea of what she was going through.

"So, what is it?" I questioned her.

Before she replied, she was quiet again. Looking at me, she said, "it's a rare genetic disease; it is lethal in 50% of the people who contract it. They don't have a known cure, some people just fight their way through it, and some people don't."

"Oh Sue," I moaned. "That's awful. I'm so, so sorry you have to go through this."

"Me too" she said. "They have developed a drug that I just started taking; it's an experimental drug that is supposed to attack the gene that causes the disease."

"Sometimes I feel so high that I can actually reach the sky." She grinned.

"Huh. So, you ended up learning to fly. Ha ha."

"I guess I did." She agreed with me.

"Yes she's flying, afraid to fall"

"I'm afraid of the future."

Those simple words hit me like a brick upside the head. I'm positive that it was at that exact second that I knew what Sue was experiencing; she was being affected by a force that she had no control over, something so diabolical that it had to have been calamitous to have to face.

Additionally, it seemed that she had no safety net into which she could tumble; no one there to hold her hand, give her a hug, comfort her during her ordeal.

I realized that Sue was under much more pressure than I could ever have recognized. No wonder she was not happy, no wonder she was acting that everything was okay in her life when the exact opposite was true.

"Is there anything they can do to help?" I inquired. "The Doctors, I mean." I added unnecessarily.

"Well, like I said, they have started me on an experimental drug that has had success in other patients. I'm keeping my fingers crossed."

"How long have you been taking it?"

"I started the drug regime approximately three weeks ago."

"Have you noticed any difference so far?" I quizzed her like a science teacher with a recalcitrant middle school student.

"No. Not yet." She countered.

"Is there anything I can do to help?" I asked in helpless fashion.

She fielded the question with aplomb. "Not really, Harry."

"How are you handling it?"

"I'm still here," she acknowledged.

"Now I feel bad." I rejoined.

"It's not your fault," she answered. "You had no influence whatsoever on me getting this disease."

"I'll tell you why baby's crying"

Sue started to softly cry.

"It will be okay Sue," I told her. I reached across the front seat and folded her into my arms. I patted her back in a consoling manner. "It's okay."

"I just want someone to listen to me, to hold me, to care about what I am going through." She sobbed into my shoulder.

"I'm here for you mylady."

"What if I die? Harry? I'm not ready for that. I'm too young to be done."

I did not know how to respond, this had all happened so quickly, it was like a tsunami wave that suddenly hit a sun-bleached beach under a clear blue sky. My heart pitter-pattered anxiously, while my brain worked feverishly to provide coherent words, comforting phrases of love and hope.

For the first time in my life, I was at a loss for something to say.

In my defense, I had never been faced with a situation like this in my lifetime. Come to think of it, I sincerely hoped that I would never have to be faced with a scenario such as this ever again; I don't believe I had ever felt so exposed, so feeble, my feelings so handcuffed.

I continued to hold her as her tears slowly subsided. I listened while her mewings competed against the rain still drumming against the roof of the taxi.

"I truly believe that you will survive this, in fact, I have to believe that because you are correct; you are much too young to be taken away from us."

Sue sniffled. "Thank you, Harry.

"Cause she's dying, aren't we all"

Sue was flying high above the radar and was afraid that a fall would mean her demise. I thought to myself, 'she really is far too young for an early death'.

She was in the process of dying and I didn't know what to do. Of course, aren't we all dying to some degree or the other? Or, is that just the poet within me espousing thoughts that poets espouse?

I don't know, I'm not sure of anything regarding this entire episode. The evening had started in such a positive way; even with the rain steadily falling, I had conducted reliable business throughout the day, I had made money, and then I had found the love of my life in the back of my taxi. That's when it all came crashing down.

As Sue continued to tremble in my arms, mad thoughts coursed their way through my head, bouncing from one side to the other attempting to dislodge me from the even keel I had always maintained.

143

I could not believe that I had just found Sue once again, only to discover that the possibility existed that I would lose her forever.

Of course, it could be that it was supposed to be that way; that she was meant to touch my life at only certain junctures, and that at those junctures her influence on me would be at its very strongest.

"Is it fate?" I whispered into her ear.

Her tears had stopped. She lifted her head and wiped her eyes. "Do you mean is it fate that we found each other once again?"

"That is exactly what I mean."

She echoed me as she pulled away from my embrace. She looked me in the eye. "Well if that is exactly what you mean, then yes, it probably is our destiny. We are all slated to die at some point, right?"

I could not tell if she was angry or resigned about her deathly situation.

I tread carefully as I pondered my reply; I was cognizant that I had little idea or concept as to how she was coping with the fact that she might die. I wanted to be sympathetic, or at least empathetic, and I surely did not wish to seem to be a jerk.

"I wish I could do something, anything at all, to help you."

"You can Harry! You can be the best man that you can possibly be. I love the fact that you are willing to drive a taxi cab while you struggle towards your goal of fame and fortune. I want you to achieve your objectives! I want you to become a famous singer. I want to hear you on WOLD every hour, on the hour. I want you to write and sing your songs and be famous!"

"You can do it Harry. I know you can, I've always known that you can. I left you so that you could accomplish the success that I know you can achieve."

I searched her face, amazed at her exuberance and passion.

I was literally in shock; it has been an evening of surprise, shock, joy, happiness, sadness, compassion, and hope all rolled into one. The myriad of feelings roiling throughout my being left me breathless.

I could not think of anything else to say to her as Sue sat back in her seat. She pulled the visor down to look in the mirror. She dabbed at her eyes with a tissue that she pulled from her purse.

Glancing at me, she said "we should probably get going. I know you are working."

I smiled. "You are the last fare for my night" I told her.

"Oh," she replied. "Well, I need to get home."

"Okay," I agreed. "Never let it be said that I failed on my gentlemanly duties."

"Yeah, right." She laughed. "You are a taxi driver, that's how you make your money."

I laughed at her teasing words. We had spent the last hour together and it seemed as if we had never parted. I did not want to think about it, but I was in a quandary; since I had found Sue, I did not really wish to lose her all over again.

"There was not much more for us to talk about"

I wanted to say something, but did not know what to say or how to approach the subject, so I was silent.

So was Sue.

I wondered if we had anything else to say to each other. The silence was more comfortable than disconcerting however, and that allowed both of us to sink into our own thoughts.

I watched as the rain outside slowed once again, no longer the deluge that it was earlier in the evening. The wind blew off the ocean and through my cracked window, bringing with it the sharp, acidic odor that always seemed to follow any of the Pacific storms.

I drove the rain-soaked roads, watching carefully for standing water and aware of the resulting glare off the puddles.

Sue was just as quiet as myself.

We both maintained our silence, it was
not an anxious stillness, more a taciturnity
of understanding, a reticence between two
comparable souls, soulmates if you will;
two individuals who were comfortable
enough with one another that they felt no
need to express their verbal thoughts.

I wondered if she felt the same way as I,
but I did not feel a compulsion to discover
the truth of the matter by breaking the
quiescence.

I continued my driving looking for
Parkside Lane.

"Whatever we had once was gone"

As I contemplated our future, or our lack of a future, I wondered if Sue and I would ever meet again, if our paths would cross, if our ships would meet as if in a convoy being breached by a Chinese merchant ship in the middle of the night with a resulting crash that would completely flatten the hull of our ship.

Was what Sue and I once shared never to be shared again? Seriously? That shouldn't be possible after a night like tonight. The prospect weighed upon me heavily.

"Penny for your thoughts" Sue's voice broke my reverie.

I waited before I responded. "I was wondering if we would ever meet again." My voice may have sounded melancholy though I tried my best to keep my emotions in check."

Sue reached across the seat and patted my arm, "we will see each other again Harry, I promise you that."

"How can you know that?" I asked her roughly.

"Harry!" She exclaimed. "Do you not know that we are supposed to meet in the future? Do you not know that you and I were supposed to meet tonight? It was our kismet! It was meant to be."

I laughed out loud. "Even with your situation Sue, you still know how to make me laugh, how to make me smile, how to make me feel good. Thank you, Sue." I told her. "It means the world to me."

We smiled at each other and enjoyed the camaraderie, complicit in the knowledge that whatever we used to have was gone, but comfortable with the fact that perhaps the future was even brighter than the past.

"So, I turned my cab into the driveway"

Parkside Lane was coming up on the righthand side, and I slowed the vehicle as I approached the street. This was quite obviously the richest part of town, and the solitude was only overcome by the monied atmosphere.

After turning south, I searched for 1600. I finally found it and turned into the driveway. Before I had gone more than 50 yards, I was stopped by a closed wrought iron gate. Next to the gate was an electronic voice box with buttons that allowed for two-way communication.

I pressed the top button and spoke into the speaker.

"Taxi services" I looked at Sue inquiringly. "Name?" I mouthed to her.

"It's Sue" she spoke up from the seat. "Please open the gate."

We waited for a moment until with a lurch, the gate began to roll back, allowing access to my vehicle.

"Past the gate and the fine trimmed lawns"

I entered the estate and directed the taxi down the long driveway. I drove slowly and carefully.

Now that the bright moon had chased the clouds and rain away, there was plenty of light to view the mansion ahead and the surrounding yards and buildings.

The view was breathtaking and impressive. The lawns were manicured as if with a nail clipper and the bushes were equal in stature.

A full-time gardener (or two) likely had the responsibility of maintaining the lawns, and were excellent at their duties. I had viewed lawns similar to these on previous visits to this side of town, but now that I actually knew someone who resided in one of these residences, I looked more critically at the extravagances; especially since I knew that the aforementioned resident did not give one hoot about the house, lawns or other occupants.

"And she said we must get together"

I drove the cab slowly towards the massive front door and slowed down in an appropriate and slow manner; the perfect taxi cab driver with the perfect passenger sitting imperfectly in the front seat.

As I rolled the conveyance to a halt adjacent to the front door, I turned to Sue to thank her for a wonderful evening.

"This was nice Sue," I told her. "I have never had a deeper conversation or a better interaction with any other passenger in my conveyance whatsoever.

Thank you." I said these words as sincerely as I possibly could, and meant every syllable that I spoke.

She leaned across the seat and gave me a peck on the cheek.

"Harry," she said, "be good. Accomplish your goals, achieve your objectives, dream your dreams and then make them come true. Remember, I believe in you."

"Thank you so much Sue, you have changed my life again! You will never know how happy that makes me feel," I told her. "I want you to know that I will always love you. I will always be grateful to you."

"You know Harry, we really should get together again."

"But I knew it'd never be arranged"

I looked at her and had an epiphany, we likely would never see each other again. After this evening, we would part ways and like two ships in the middle of the ocean; we could search through the thousands of miles of undulating ocean waves, never to cross each other's paths ever again.

I knew right then that it would never be arranged; that if it was to happen it would happen. But, I knew it'd never be arranged per se, instead it would be at the whim of fate, much like tonight's episode.

What worried me, well, bothered me more than worried me, the most, was that there was a distinct possibility that after tonight the next time I viewed this beautiful and artistic women, it might be through the eyes of death. The thought was disturbing to say the least and depressing would be a much better description.

How many times in life would a chance to interact with the one individual on the planet who could or would influence me without undue pressure ever happen without it being arranged?

That was not the thought that I wanted to have careening around my skull, but it was there without any effort on my part to contain it.

It was just another thought on this very strange evening that threatened to either embolden me with reserve, courage and strength, or (once I dropped off my beautiful passenger) overcome me with emotion and pain that could knock me off this precarious perch called life.

I looked at the massive front door; the fact that it stood closed even though someone had to have noticed that the taxi from the front gate had arrived, bothered me immensely. It seemed symbolic of the entire evening; a door to the travails to Sue's life, it still remained closed to me.

The entire night had a strange effect on me; in fact, the entire day was quite strange now that I think about it. I knew that it would be raining hard throughout the day, I knew that I needed money and would have to work, but I had hoped to have enough free time to work on a new song. Instead I got caught up in various tasks that caused me to be late to work, it had already started to rain, I was in an ambivalent mood, yet that all changed as soon as I picked up my women in blue.

The soaring feeling of elation that was experienced as I discovered the identity of my passenger was only equaled by the debby-downer feeling experienced by discovering that she was dying. The two extremes were just too incompatible.

It was too much to take in, in was too incomprehensible, in was too exhausting. I couldn't handle the emotions; they were just too much for me.

I turned to Sue.

"And she handed me twenty dollars, for a two-fifty fare"

Before I could open my mouth to explain to Sue the conflicting emotions besetting my soul, she reached into her handbag and pulled out a small, pink wallet decorated with tiny diamonds that winked mysteriously in the moonlight.

She opened the wallet, reached inside and pulled out a twenty-dollar bill. Folding it in half, she handed the money to me.

I looked at her in amazement. "What's this for?" I exclaimed in surprise.

She started to chuckle. "Harry, that's for the ride home." She pointed to the meter connected to the dashboard; it blinked steadily in bright red numbers "2.50".

I realized that she was paying her fare for the taxi ride. "Oh," I responded weakly. "I forgot."

"Well, you aren't a very good taxi-cab driver then, now are you?"

I laughed out loud, in a relieved kind of way.

"I totally forgot that you were a passenger," I told her.

"Well, it's a good thing that I did not."

She paused for a second before continuing. "I meant what I said Harry, I want you to go forth into the world, continue your endeavors, and believe in yourself. If you promise me that you will do that, I will die a happy woman."

My breath caught in my throat and a tear grew in my eye then slid down my cheek. Even now, Sue cared more about me and my future than she did about herself, her goals, and her objectives. Now, that was true love.

She wiped the tear from my cheek, then pressed her fingers to her mouth. She sucked on the tips of her fingers then reached across the seat and pulled my head towards hers. She kissed me lightly on the lips then pulled away.

"She said, "Harry keep the change"

"I have only one more thing to tell you Harry," she said playfully.

"What's that?" I asked in anticipation.

"Harry, keep the change!"

I laughed out loud. "Sue, it's only a $2.50 fare, you don't have to tip me that much."

"I don't have to, I know that. But, I do want to. So, just keep it."

"Now, another man might have been angry, and another man might have been hurt"

I looked at her in consternation.

"Seriously, Sue. You don't have to give me that much."

"Seriously Harry," she mimicked me. "I know exactly what I am doing. Keep the money, do with it what you will. I have plenty, and what else am I supposed to do with it. If I did not think that you had too much pride, I would offer you a lot more."

"I don't know if that is a compliment or not," I protested. "How am I supposed to take that?"

"It's okay, Harry. If I did not want to do so, believe me I wouldn't."

I sat back in my seat and studied her features. Who was this creature with a heart of gold? Should I be angry with her that she thought she had to provide me with such largesse?

Should I have my feelings hurt? Should I feel disgruntled due to my pride? I don't think so; I don't think she meant any more by her action than a gesture of kindness, but what does it mean to a man when a woman whom he loves (or at least used to love) pities him in such a manner?

I could not decide what my exact response should be. I was stupefied; there have been relatively few instances when a passenger has provided me with such a large tip, and most of the time they were drunk or stoned.

I did not mind taking large tips in those circumstances were my passengers were inebriated or high, because most of the time those passengers were the most difficult to handle. Oftentimes, they puked all over my cab, or even worse, left other strange, smelly gifts for me in the back seat.

This situation was entirely different. Sue was not drunk or stoned or a sexual miscreant carrying on loudly and obnoxiously in the back of my taxi.

Instead Sue was by far and away the most beautiful, compassionate, caring and loving passenger I had ever had the honor to escort from one side of San Francisco to the other.

"But another man never would have let her go"

I looked at the twenty-dollar bill that Sue had pressed into my hand. Then I glanced upward into Sue's eyes to see what I could behold there. What I saw pained my more than anything I could have ever experienced. She was gazing at me with such love and devotion that her face and eyes shone with an inner radiance that could best be described as divine.

I asked myself, "Harry, what are you doing? Why are you letting this truly tremendous woman out of your life? Are you really that coarse? Are you truly that unaware of what this woman could do for you?

Obviously, she loves you more than you will ever know or understand, why can't you just accept that, reach out to her, take her in your arms, hold her tight and never, never, never let her go?"

Those are all questions that I asked myself, and I truly did not have a reasonable answer.

It was a very disheartening acceptance of knowledge that I might be making the biggest mistake of my life; a mistake that I would be repeating since I had already made that same mistake years and years ago back in Newark.

Had I truly not progressed at all? Of course, I could be reading this all wrong, right?

"I stashed the bill in my shirt"

Making a fateful decision; I folded the twenty-dollar bill in half once again and placed it carefully and nonchalantly into my shirt pocket.

"Thank you, Sue," I told her. "For everything."

A flash of disappointment crossed her eyes in an instant. Or perhaps, I had just imagined it. Whichever it was, she patted my cheek once again, reached down and opened the car door.

The door squeaked loudly in protest, and I grimaced. I really did need to get that door oiled. The only reason why I was thinking in that manner was because I was doing my best to distract myself from the situation at hand and the barbarous mistake that I was committing.

She carefully reached her leg out the door and felt for the ground beneath her. Not wishing to step into a puddle or a quagmire of mud, she looked intently at the direction she was stepping.

I leaped from my side of the cab, and grabbed her packages that she had left. Before she could move away from the cab, I hurried to her side with the bags and boxes.

"Here you go Sue," I stammered.

Smiling at me in a whimsical manner, she took the proffered packages and settled them into her arms. Sue turned away and again I felt a sense of loss that threatened my very being.

"And she walked away in silence"

As she turned away, my hand came up to pull her back. Before I could follow through on that action, I let my hand drop back down to my side.

My song was bubbling to the surface and I had another line to add to what was quickly becoming the eulogy that I would never wish to give.

I thought to myself in poetic justice "and she walked away in silence". Yet, I did nothing at all to stop her except stand there and watch as she walked towards the door.

I hoped against hope that she would be stronger (or perhaps weaker) than I, turn around and come running back to me with packages strewn behind her and arms open wide to embrace me. Alas, that was not to be, instead, the romantic heart beating within me, continued to carry on its rhythmic cries. I did nothing to alleviate the pain and confusion those cries caused.

"It's strange, how you never know"

Life is really, really, strange. This morning I had awakened with no other cares in my heart, or worries in my head other than writing my next song, organizing my next gig, and driving my taxi to cover my living expenses.

Now, here I was standing outside one of the biggest mansions I had ever laid eyes on, watching my one true love walk away in silence.

I not only find out that she was quite possibly dying, but that she had sent me away on purpose when we were young because she thought she would hold me back from the special purpose that she discerned within me.

Trust me to make the same mistake not just once in my life, but twice. Would I never learn?

I guess I could take the next line to my song, and apply it quite aptly to my own life. "It's strange how you never know," I thought to myself.

How life turns out is often a surprise to us. I wonder if there really is a God and if so, what his sense of humor must be. Because it seems to me that he must think he is a real funny guy.

God is not, but it does seem that way sometimes. He sets us up with situations out of our control, and then allows us to make decisions on our own that dictate our focus, our footfalls along the pathway which we choose, and the troubles which we encounter are usually troubles that we have brought upon ourselves.

It's just a real strange life we live.

"But, we both gotten what we asked for
Such a long long time ago"

Life is strange, that's for sure. If you think about it though, both Sue and I had gotten what we had asked for such a long, long time ago.

As I stood there watching Sue walk away in silence, I contemplated where we were after this evening's events. I also thought about how we had started our lives in a quiet little suburb community of Newark, how we both traveled wildly different routes to get us to the exact same spot on the planet, at this exact moment in time.

I can only describe the mixed emotions of the evening, the feeling of what was going to be no matter what, and how we are destined at certain times in our lives to meet up with the specific, and perfect, individual who will help us the most at that time in our lives with the exact problem we need help the most with.

Do you understand where I am coming from? If you do it's probably a good thing, because I'm not sure that I even understand. I told you earlier that it had been a strange night, and all this heavy thinking about life, and fate, and destiny, and fortune, and hope, and cheer, and especially Sue, is a bit much for me.

If it wasn't supposed to take place, then it would not have taken place. So, I guess I better suck it up and get on with life.

Wait a minute, you say? You want a more complete explanation of what I mean? Ok, here goes!

"You see, she was going to be an actress, and I was going to learn to fly"

Remember early in this story when I told you that Sue's dream and desire was to become an actress, and not just any old movie star, but a true legend of greatness?

Do you also remember that I was going to learn to fly?

Okay, well just to remind you; when Sue and I first started going out, learning about love, learning to share our thoughts, our dreams, our goals, our objectives, our very desires by sharing our most secret thoughts and emotions.

We fell in love. Maybe some of you would describe it as puppy love, and maybe deep inside our own hearts we may not have known exactly what we had together, but we both knew that we shared something special.

Sue confided in me her most sincere desire to be an actress, and I confided in her my most ardent desire to learn to fly.

"She took off to find the footlights
I took off for the sky"

Do you still not recognize the irony of the actions and events that we both went through; Sue leaving Newark to find the Hollywood fame and fortune she truly desired, and me leaving for Colorado and the beautiful mountains in which I would soon be flying?

Perhaps I should fill you in a little more so that you can understand the picture more completely. Not that I think you are a dullard, or that you haven't fully engaged your brain, but the obvious is biting you in the butt, and you may not even realize it.

Maybe if I emboldened the key words involving the scenario, you could jump right on it.

Sue was going to be an **ACTRESS**

I was going to learn to **FLY**

"And here she's acting happy inside her handsome home"

I guess I will just come right out and say it to you, Sue is *acting happy* inside her handsome home. She is acting. She's not happy, she may not have ever been happy.

Instead, Sue could quite possible die far too young, and way before she could quit acting like she's happy, and just go be happy.

I felt sorry for her. Here she was in a huge fashionable mansion, with servants to care for her every need, yet none cared enough to even discern her unhappiness.

I watched as the door opened and an older man in a butler suit stood inside to assist Sue as she entered. She never turned, and why should she say goodbye to the taxi-cab driver? I was just one more secret in her long list of secrets.

I turned back to my vehicle and climbed inside.

"And me, I'm flying in my taxi"

I started the engine that I had shut off, and listened to the rumble before putting it in gear.

What's that you say? You still don't get how I'm flying? You think I'm just a common, ordinary, everyday taxi-cab driver?

Well, let me tell you something friend; every single day that I drive my taxi…I'm flying. Yep, that's right, I'm flying in my taxi.

Still don't have any clue as to what exactly I'm referring to? Well, that's disturbing.

You see there are plenty of times when I'm all alone in my cab, and I can do as I please, especially if I leave the window down with a cleansing wind blowing through the entire vehicle, if you catch my drift.

"Taking tips, and getting stoned"

Right about now, you most likely think I'm crazy, but I'm not. Not even close to that.

I will try to help you out by being more specific about what I mean. Read my words again; I'm in my taxi, taking tips and getting stoned. Both actions can lead to flying, or at least a sense of elation about a job well done. That's especially true when you receive a $20 bill for a $2.50 fare.

There is no greater feeling of joy and self-fulfillment that can be had than to receive a gratuity that denotes the fact that you are a special individual, or at the very least, in one person's eyes, you provided a very special service.

Do I have to be more specific than that?

*"I go flying so high, when I'm **stoned**."*

My song is completed.

THE END

www.ingramcontent.com/pod-product-compliance
Lightning Source LLC
Chambersburg PA
CBHW071246130626
46556CB00003B/1183